A KISS FROM A MERMAN

KISS FROM A MONSTER SERIES
BOOK 8

CHARLOTTE SWAN

eBook ISBN:

978-1-960615-19-0

Paperback ISBN:

978-1-960615-20-6

Cover Design by Charlotte Swan

www.authorcharlotteswan.com

 Formatted with Vellum

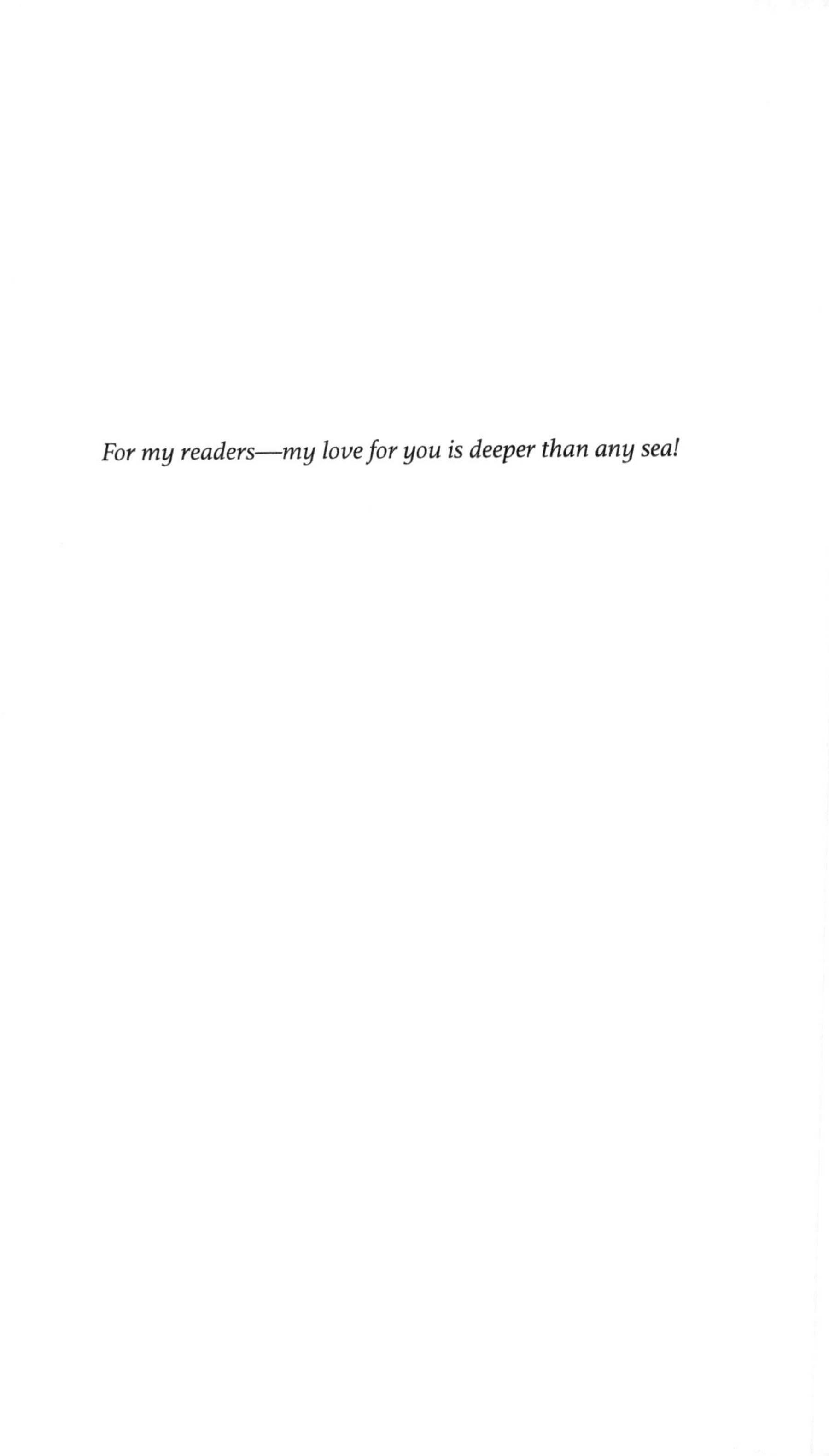

For my readers—my love for you is deeper than any sea!

CONTENT WARNINGS

For a full list of content and trigger warnings please go to the author's website.
www.authorcharlotteswan.com

ASTRYD

If only I had left town sooner, I could've avoided this entire situation.

It was foolish to think the unrest permeating the town over the last few months wouldn't affect me. I believed the worst thing I would have to endure was a cutting of my wages at the bakery. Customers had become scarce due to the troubles on the high seas.

Stories of sinking ships and drowned sailors were carried by the handful of vessels that had safely made port in Bluewater. The villagers of this modest-sized trading town depended on the fleet of ships to bring in fish and goods from other lands. If the fish markets weren't thriving, then the people of Bluewater would suffer.

The last whole fish was sold over three weeks ago. The only thing left in the market's crates were handfuls of mussels and shrimps, and even those had begun to dwindle. People had taken to cooking and eating the seaweed that washed ashore. When the markets began to dry up, there was a noticeable shift in the villagers.

Still, like a fool, I believed things would turn around. We

only needed a few fruitful deliveries to make landfall, and order would return to our town. As supplies became scarcer, I knew Gil would have a harder time justifying my job at Sugarfish Bakery. It wouldn't have been ideal to find myself jobless, but I had my savings I could live on. People were fleeing the city at an exorbitant rate, so there was no real danger of being evicted from my apartment.

I had no family—no parents or husband. There were no hungry mouths of children I was responsible for feeding. In comparison, I was lucky, but that luck would soon run out. I knew the people of Bluewater were getting desperate for a solution.

However, I never imagined that desperation would lead them straight to a madman.

To a swashbuckling, pirate captain who had pillaged and ransacked every land he had visited. His reputation preceded him—he was ruthless and not to be trusted. Yet, that is exactly what the people of Bluewater did. They welcomed this viper into their home, where he hatched a plan he promised would save us all.

Those most desperate had looked at him like he was a god —a savior sent to spare them from their plight. What he said made sense to those who were hungry and hopeless. Captain Blacktide said the way to bring peace back to the riotous seas was easy: we had to appease the Kraken.

Blacktide said the monster beneath the waves had not taken a human bride in some time. Growing up by the sea, we had all been taught the legend of the Kraken as a cautionary tale to not stray from our beds at night. It was an old wives' tale, and yet, it rang like prophecy through the town. The Kraken was angry, and he was sinking the ships carrying food and supplies as punishment—it seemed as logical an answer as any to the starving masses of Bluewater.

To stop his anger, all we had to do was offer up a human

sacrifice as his bride. When this suggestion was first made a few weeks ago, many in the village had rejected the captain's sentiments. However, as hunger worsened and madness became easier to catch than scurvy, more people began to listen to him in earnest.

After all, what was it to sacrifice one in order to save everyone?

I hadn't given much thought to any of it—I had survived this long on stale bread and used teabags. Before my parents passed, we had fallen on hard times. It was never pleasant, but it taught me that all struggles eventually come to an end. Besides, the only way out of Bluewater was to set off through *The Woods*. If the Kraken was meant to keep children in their beds, *The Woods* was meant to ensure they never put even one toe into the treeline. Legend or not, the tales of the creatures dwelling inside made me unwilling to venture through something I was sure would blow over in a month's time.

It was my ignorance and fear that led me straight to the pirate captain.

Captain Blacktide had never taken note of me. A fact, I was grateful for, given his reputation. In Bluewater, I filtered through the crowd like any other unremarkable fish in a school of others. It wasn't until last night, when I was coming home late from my final shift at the bakery, that I passed by him, speaking to his supporters.

They were whipped into a frenzy under the torches they carried. Foam collected between their cracked lips as their dazed eyes regarded the captain as a deity. His mouth was spewing the same sermon he had given for the last five weeks. I had pulled my cloak tighter around myself and hurried my steps. Only it didn't matter; I had been spotted, and the life I knew ended in the blink of an eye.

"You there," Captain Blacktided had called. "Girl. Come here."

I had swallowed and walked faster only to be snagged around the arms by two burly figures. With swords at their hips, I had no chance of fighting them. They dragged me toward Captain Blacktide, who had them rip my cloak off me. His eyes gleamed as did his one gold tooth. Licking over his cracked lips, he surveyed my body despite my attempts to cover it.

"You—you will do. A beautiful bride for the Kraken," Captain Blacktided declared, pointing a long, ring-addled finger at me. "Who knows this young woman?"

I prayed for silence, but a voice from the crowd rang out.

"She works at Gil's. An orphan. Unmarried."

I glared towards the crowd, their hungry faces stared back at me with no remorse. They no longer saw me as one of them. I was a pawn to be used in their own salvation. Anything I said would not be heard. I couldn't fight them—I couldn't go home; they'd tear my building down to get to me.

The quiet, solitary life I had carefully crafted for myself was gone. In hindsight, I should've tried to fight. To break away and make a run for it, just to say I did. It wouldn't have made much of a difference. The evening would've unfolded the same way, albeit I probably would've been more bruised.

"It is decided then. We will give her to the Kraken at dawn." Captain Blacktide's eyes darkened. "Are you a virgin, dear?"

My cheeks had heated at the indignant question. Even with my freedom dwindling, I still held onto my pride.

"No," I had said, willing my face not to betray the lie.

Captain Blacktide sucked in a breath, shaking his head before waving a dismissive hand.

"It matters little. You will be our human sacrifice. No one is to touch her." He nodded once more to his men. "Take her to the dungeons."

And the dungeons are where I spent my last night of freedom. I was given a singular cup of wine and pieces of dried fish.

Sleep had not come easily on the stone bench I was meant to lie on. My jailers roused me an hour ago and stripped me of my gown. Trembling in my thin shift, I hadn't even tried to fight them. My body had gone completely numb.

I barely registered the sight of the massive rock as Captain Blacktide and his pirates rowed me out towards it. The rising sun glowed along the bright blue water. The pirate captain reeked of whiskey and body odor as he unloaded me from the boat. Heavy iron shackles were placed around my wrists and ankles.

"Your death will not be in vain. Remember that," Blacktide said before stepping back into his boat, leaving me bound to the massive boulder.

That is where I am now, contemplating the choices that have led me here.

The sun rose high overhead, and the heat beat down on me with a burning intensity. Salt stung my nostrils. A few seagulls called overhead. It has only been a few hours, but the sea is already rising. When I was initially placed here, it lapped gently at my ankles. Now, the brackish water has reached my chest.

No Kraken is coming for me. I will drown before all the villagers standing along the docks, barely a hundred yards away. Not one of them will save me. They won't risk the pirate's ire, but more importantly, they want what he has said to be true. They'd rather have me live a life of eternal pain if it meant ending their own suffering.

Desperation dances in their hungry eyes as they stare out at me. My mouth is parched, and I don't bother using my last minutes of air to call out to them. It would be useless.

My eyes snag on a familiar face near the front of the dock. Gil's green eyes are framed with deep wrinkles. When our gazes lock, he swiftly looks away, and my heart cracks. He is not my family, even though he had taken me in at sixteen, shortly after my parents' deaths. I had started looking up to him. I thought he cared enough about me that he would've spoken up on my behalf. Even if it had only been the barest of condemnation, it would've meant the world to me.

Yet, as I watch him clutch the hands of his two young sons, I realize just how wrong I had been. Gil has his own family to take care of. I have no one. No one will mourn me, no one will miss me. I have spent the last eight years alone, and I will die alone.

Nothing like being chained to a rock against the rising tide to make one realize how inconsequential they are.

Sweat pours down my neck, and the water rises even higher. It brushes the underside of my chin. My arms have gone numb from being chained above my head. The skin on my shoulders is red from the sun. My throat feels like sand. The edges of my vision begin to blur.

From the dock, I can hear a few murmurs. An older woman, draped in stained linen, thrusts a bony hand towards me.

"Is this right? She will drown soon?"

"Why has he not come?" a young man beside her asks.

"Patience," Blacktide snarls. "He will come. Have faith."

Have faith.

There was a time I believed in something bigger than myself. I had dreams of adventures—of setting off in one of the ships that docked in the harbor and seeing what the world had to offer. Now, as I feel the sea bathe my lips, I realize I was always on borrowed time.

Bluewater is not kind to unaccompanied females. Still, to die at twenty-four at the behest of a madman seems ridiculously unfair. If I live through this, I will live each day for myself. I'd have adventures—I wouldn't hold myself back. Dreams of what could've been dance through my mind and distract me from the fact that the water has now reached my nose.

"What's that?" someone calls from the dock.

"Did you see it?"

"Have faith!"

The water covers my nose, and I let go. With one final silent plea, my weightless body remains tethered to the rock as the last dregs of air still in my lungs. I pray that this is over swiftly and that in the next life I'm dealt a kinder hand. A few more voices rise up, but I don't hear them. My vision blurs, and everything goes dark.

2

QURILL

I've lingered in this bay for far too long.

It's been nearly a year since I returned to my father's palace, and based on his correspondence, my growing absence is displeasing my mother. And whatever brings my mother anything less than joy, my father will deal with swiftly. Even though I know I should leave, my restless spirit bids me to linger in Bluewater Bay a bit longer.

The water here is calmer than the waves at the heart of the Darksea. The outbreak of riotous water and darkening skies has nothing to do with my father or me. The sea is its own entity, with powers far beyond all our comprehension. It exacts revenge on the sailors it deems necessary to pay its watery tithe. Even my father is a servant to the water—no one commands him more than the tides.

Well, one person does. My mother.

My heart pangs at the thought of them. The ache is a familiar one. Our relationship has grown fraught recently, which is why I've been delaying my return home. I know they only want what's best for me. Is it not in a son's nature to rebel? The weight of their expectation feels like an anchor around my ankle. I'm only thirty-five, and the thought of settling down makes me itch. Monotony to me is a fate worse than death.

My father had lived for centuries before finding my mother. For her part, she had years as Queen of the Darksea before I came into the picture. They both had their adventures—albeit together—and they want the same for me.

They worry about me being alone, but perhaps that's what I've always desired. Space. To set out on my own and flourish, living by no rules except the ones I set for myself. It's why I've remained in residence at Sunshell Palace for all this time, away from their prying eyes and gentle urgings.

If I'm being honest, the time out here has begun to lose its sparkle. I envy my parents' love—anyone would. It would be a dream to find that sort of connection for myself one day. They would be very displeased to learn how I've spent my nights: donning the physique of a human man and debauching myself with any human I could find up and down the coastline. The pleasure had been great, but after each interaction, I couldn't help but feel like I was missing something.

I would hate to admit that my parents were right—that I was lonely. However, how could I find someone to fit more permanently into my life? My father had taken my mother against her will. She came to love him quickly and gave up her human life to be with him eternally. Was there another such woman out there for me who would be willing to make the same sacrifice?

If there was, I certainly hadn't found her yet. I had never been with a human in my true form—the sentiments expressed by many of them were that my kind were decidedly unwelcome.

The golden sun glows brightly overhead. The heat warms my scales as I sun myself on a floating piece of driftwood. My mind is made up as I breathe in the salty air. This will be my last day here. In the morning, I will return to my parents' palace and face the questions about my future head-on.

I have neglected my royal duties as Prince of the Darksea for long enough.

A flash of white glimmers on the horizon. Sliding into the water, my vision catches on a protruding rock. The waves have nearly completely swallowed it. Humans linger on the dock staring at the rock with determination. I haven't drifted this far down the bay in some time. I prefer to stick to the more rural shanty towns rather than take my chances in the populated city.

The villagers point at the rock, and my curiosity is piqued. Diving beneath the water, I quickly swim over to the boulder. It's far enough away that none of them can reach me if I surface.

As I approach, my eyes widen at the sight beneath the waves. Thin white fabric floats around two delicate knees. Heavy iron chains lock around two slender ankles.

Waves lap at her nose. The young woman's face is nearly completely submerged in the water. Her golden hair floats around her like a halo. What is the meaning of all this? The scene before me makes no sense.

Through the water, voices float to me from the dock. A merman's hearing is unparalleled.

"There must be something wrong with her," a woman's voice spits.

"Or the Kraken has truly forsaken us, and even a human bride won't appease him," a deeper voice offers.

"Whatever the case," the woman responds, "it is a pity to lose a girl so young. Blacktide will have much to answer for."

A sacrifice for my father? He would not want such a thing. Not to mention my mother would be enraged at the treatment of this poor girl. She looks asleep, her head lulls against the rock as the waves cover her face completely. Whoever she is, she is beautiful.

I must act fast.

Slicing through the water, I make quick work of breaking apart the bindings around her ankles. The water slides down my body as I plant my feet next to hers. There are a few gasps that ring out behind me, but I pay them little mind. The human's lips have gone blue. With a growl, I summon a wave to cover us from the prying eyes of the villagers.

Making quick work of the biddings on her wrists, her delicate arms fall limply to her sides. Without her tether, she falls into my open arms. She weighs nothing, lighter than a rainbow fish. Her skin glows—as luminous as a deep sea pearl.

She is young, but a girl she is certainly not. Golden skin greets my eyes. Her body is all soft curves. The fullness of her chest and hips and the slight curve of her stomach are on display in her soaked shift. I can nearly make out the shade of pink her nipples are. I snarl at myself. There is no time for gawking.

I can admire her beauty more when she begins to draw breath.

The faint pattering of her heart reminds me of the task at hand. Angry welts decorate her shoulders. The tip of her upturned nose is crimson. The skin around her wrists and ankles is red, irritated by the salt water. They'll need to be cleaned to avoid infection.

Using my magic, I summon the water from her lungs, drawing it out and through her full lips. She chokes, coughing awake as she spits up the salty water. Once it is out and she's breathing deeply again, I marvel at the sight of her once more. Eyes the color of sapphires stare back at me. They are wary but not afraid.

She has not removed my arms from around her, but to be fair, I'm not so certain she could stand on her own. The press of her body against mine is a delight. I have never seen her before. I'd remember a beauty as bewitching as hers.

Golden lashes flutter on her cheeks as she blinks at me. Cracked lips part as her tongue snakes out to lick them.

"Thank you."

Her voice is hoarse but sounds like music to me.

"You're welcome."

Searching for something better to say, I watch a serene smile come over her face. She leans back, allowing me to support her weight. With a deep breath, she drops her arms to her sides.

"I'm ready to go now. I'm ready for the pain to be over." Her blue eyes meet mine. "Will you stay with me? Until the end?"

Her words click, and protectiveness surges through me. This is not her end—far from it. The little human in my arms doesn't know it yet, but this is the beginning of the rest of her life. This powerful desire to claim her—this need to shield her from harm and provide for her is something I've never felt before. However, I've heard about these feelings all my life.

I was a different male before I found her. She's changed me in the span of a heartbeat. My father said it was instant—uncontrollable—and he was right. There is no going back for me. I happily give myself over to the woman in my arms. She will decide my fate, and I will do everything I can to show her I am a worthy choice.

"What is your name?"

"Astryd."

"Astryd," I repeat, tasting the word on my tongue.

She shivers at my voice. I feel her in my heart and weave her into my soul. Need kindles within me. We were always meant to meet—our paths were destined to cross. I want to know everything about her and for her to learn everything about me.

Her wounds give me pause. Once she is healed, I will set

about wooing her. For now, she needs the attention and care of my magic.

"Listen to me, Astryd. You aren't going to die." Golden brows lower over her blue eyes, but I press on. "I promise everything will be better very soon."

Unable to help myself, my fingers trail the smooth curve of her cheek. *My Astryd. Mine.* Possessiveness crowds my chest and tips my words with a deadly edge.

"And the man who chained you to this rock will be dead come sunrise."

3

———

ASTRYD

My first thought as I peel back my heavy eyelids is that I'm dead.

I drowned attached to that rock. Vague memories of a savior and crisp air were just figments of my imagination. Scenes conjured up from the depths of my mind meant to comfort me until I reached this place. Wherever I was now, there was no pain—no intense burning from the sun or chafing shackles. I was at peace, lying atop a cloud.

Everything was shockingly blue. Shimmering glass was above me. Just beyond it, schools of rainbow fish swam leisurely through open water. The image gave me pause. Glass? A school of fish? Where was I? What aquatic afterlife had I been dumped into after suffering such a watery demise?

That's when I feel it. It comes over me like a wave. Soreness radiates from every muscle. I breathe deeply, inhaling scents of sandalwood and citrus. Surely if I were dead, I would no longer need to breathe. Glancing from side to side, I realize it's not a cloud I'm lying on but a bed. One made up of silky blue sheets and large pillows. A matching silk sheet is draped over me, my naked skin sliding against the fabric with no friction.

The pain in my ankles and wrists was gone. Lifting my hand, I stare at the unmarred skin at the base of my palm. My hand lifts high, touching my shoulders that had blistered in the unforgiving sun. I gasp as the tips graze a thick gel. Swiping some of it from my shoulder, I test the green goo between my fingers. It is delightfully cool.

I return my hand to my shoulder and feel the smooth skin underneath the substance. My burns have healed just as my wrists and ankles have. How is that possible? Where am I? Unease begins to settle in as I test more gel between my fingers. I am not dead, but am I safe? Moving feels like an impossible feat and yet—

"Leave that in place."

I scream, shooting straight up on the bed at the sound of the booming voice. Apparently, fear is a good motivator. Clutching the silk sheet to my chest, my eyes widen at the figure in the doorway. Delicate green and blue scales decorate the skin of the impressive male body lingering at the threshold. Leathery blue pants cover his bottom half while his stomach and chest remain uncovered. The cuts of his muscles are impressive.

Gills protrude from his strong neck, giving way to an even firmer jaw. Fin-like ears stick out from under a thick crop of dazzling white hair. Crystal blue eyes glow in the warm light of the room. His full lips twitch before he crosses his muscular arms over his impressive chest.

My heart races. Thoughts flood my mind in a torrent. I've heard of this creature before. Sailors whisper about a rare breed of monster that hails from the depths of the sea. He is a merman.

A legend just like the Kraken, but I have seen him before.

"You saved me," I breathe, my voice hoarse from disuse.

His blue eyes flicker before nodding. Taking a small step into the room, I swallow my surprise as a plate laden with orange slices and bread appears in one hand. A glass of water appears in the other. I'm not sure what to think; my mind is a jumble of emotions. When I do not retreat further up the bed, the merman takes a few more small steps into the room.

"You need to eat. It'll help replenish your strength." He thrusts the plate towards me. "You were in pretty rough shape. It's nearly sunset, clearly you needed the rest."

Who can blame me? A dirty, cramped cell is hardly a place to catch any good sleep. I lick over my dry lips.

"Am I dead?"

I know the answer, but I need confirmation nonetheless.

"No."

I sag with relief, holding out my hand for the plate of food while keeping the other to my silk covering. Not that my modesty matters much anymore, the thin fabric cannot even conceal my hardening nipples.

"Then where am I?"

The merman purses his lips. He is only a few steps from the bed. This close, he is even more imposing. He towers over me on the lofted bed. His muscular abdomen tapers into the enticing V-shape of his hips. I've never seen a male built like this in my life. I shouldn't be noting his appealing qualities. I should be making plans to flee from wherever he's brought me.

If I'm not dead, then I still have a chance to make something of my life.

"My palace," the merman says finally, handing me the glass of water first. "Sunshell Palace to be exact. We're a few miles out from Bluewater Bay—and only a few hundred feet below the surface."

The glass freezes on my lips.

"W—we're underwater?"

My eyes fly up to the glass ceiling, to the legions of fish floating by. Coral grows along the edges. Golden sunlight pierces through the azure water. My eyes lock with the merman, who nods, setting the plate of food beside me on the bed.

"How can I breathe?"

"Drink and I'll tell you."

My thirst comes back with a vengeance. His command is one I eagerly follow.

The crisp water is cool on my tongue. Once I start, I can't seem to stop. I down one glass and then watch it magically refill. The scent of metal invades my lungs. After my third glass of water, my thirst finally wanes. I stare at the merman expectantly.

"My father ensured all the palaces in his kingdom would be conducive to human life. Our magic pumps the water out and keeps it at bay. Everything inside remains dry with fresh air to breathe."

Picking up an orange slice, I bit into nearly moaning at the sweet citrus. It has been a long time since I've been able to afford fruit, much less oranges.

"Who is your father?" I ask, reaching for another slice.

"The Kraken of the Darksea."

The sweet juice turns to ash on my tongue. A cold sweat erupts on my skin as I look up at the merman. Swallowing thickly, my heart races in my chest. It seems I'm not so lucky as to avoid death and be afforded the chance to return to my human life. That mad pirate's rantings had been correct. I was given up by my town, and now I was about to be given to a monster as his unwilling human sacrifice.

"You're taking him to me then? To be his bride?"

My voice is hollow as I drop the merman's gaze. The raging appetite I had moments ago vanishes. This nightmare has only just begun. What does a Kraken even do to a human? I shudder to think, but I guess I'll find out soon enough.

I should've drowned when I had the chance.

A soft chuckle pulls me from my dark thoughts. Looking up, the merman gazes at me as if I've grown a second head.

"Father doesn't accept human sacrifices." A soft smile curves his lips. "Or brides for that matter. My mother keeps him busy enough—he'd never take another. He loves her too fiercely for that."

The truth of his words lies bare in his eyes. I let them wash over me, smoothing away my lingering apprehension.

"Eat." The merman gestures at my plate. "Please."

I do as he says. It is easy to follow a direct command. I've had to make so many decisions in my life over the last eight years. Worries over money and the uncertainty of my future had weighed me down daily. There was no one to care for me— if I'm being honest, this merman has shown me more kindness than anyone else since my parents passed.

I'm tired of being scared. The doubt and unease have shrouded me for so long that this unbelievable situation I've found myself in feels like a reprieve. I should be scared—I should be asking to leave, but where would I return to? Bluewater is off the table. I can't go back lest they offer me up as a sacrifice again. All my belongings—not that there were many of note—and all my wages from Gil's are lost to me now.

At least I'm not alone. This is the longest I've spent in the presence of someone who wasn't Gil or a customer in years. It isn't unpleasant.

Silence settles in around us as I finish off the oranges and the loaf of bread. I slowly sip more water as the merman waves his hand. My empty plate refills. A steaming fillet of white fish coated in butter glistens next to blistered tomatoes. My stomach growls as the merman extends a fork towards me.

"Eat," he repeats. "I'll give you some space."

My heart lurches as he turns from the bed. The thought of unending silence makes my skin itch. I was a fool for not leaving Bluewater when I had the chance, and perhaps it makes me an even bigger fool for trusting this merman, but I do. He saved my life. There were plenty of chances for him to harm me—let me die. Instead, he brought me to his palace, healed me, and is now feeding me the best food I've ever had.

I want to trust him—I need to—at least for right now. Tomorrow, I will leave this place if he allows it. I'll start over somewhere new alone. Today, I'll allow myself the chance to be selfish and not let worries overwhelm me.

How much can one evening possibly change when my mind is already decided?

"Don't go," I call, as he turns from the bed.

The merman pauses, the muscles of his back tighten. Slowly, he spins back towards me, his white eyebrow raised. My cheeks heat as I shrug, spearing a piece of fish with my fork.

"I—I don't want to be alone right now."

The merman stares at me. I hold my breath, awaiting his dismissal, but it never comes. Instead, he waves his hand, and a blue upholstered chair with a high back appears. He settles his massive frame into it, the wood creaking under his weight.

Something warm floods my stomach, and I choose not to examine it too closely. I take a bite of fish. It melts on my tongue. The herb butter is beyond decadent. I devour half the fish as I feel the merman's eyes upon me. Popping a tomato into my mouth, I chew it thoughtfully before speaking.

"I remember you saving me," I confess. "I thought I was dying—that you were some entity sent to shepherd me to the afterlife."

Raw emotion flickers in his gaze.

"As I said, you were in rough shape. I nearly hadn't made it to you in time."

"Seems as though good luck finally favored me."

His gaze traces over my face.

"Mine as well."

My skin prickles with awareness. I've always been good at

avoiding attention. As a single woman, drawing too much scrutiny is never a good thing, especially in a town like Bluewater. However, I'm finding I don't mind the way the merman stares at me.

My brush with death must've robbed me of my sanity.

"What caused all of this?" he asked. "Surely the people of Bluewater aren't routinely tethering women to rocks in the middle of the sea as offerings to my father?"

I huff a humorless laugh.

"That's true. The whole human-sacrifice-to-the-Kraken thing is relatively new. Born out of starving people's desperation." Taking a sip of water, I shake my head. "Desperate people do not listen to reason. It was more logical to them to sacrifice me by believing the ravings of the mad pirate Blacktide than to find a more viable solution for the decrease in supplies at the market."

The merman's eyes widen.

"My father is not responsible for the poor luck of the sailors. The sea condemns those it chooses. Even my father is a servant to *its* will." He waves a dismissive hand, eyes narrowing in on me. "Forget all of that. No one tried to stop them? No one spoke up on your behalf? Surely your family tried to save you."

I shake my head, and a familiar sting sensation pricks my eyes.

"I'd have to have one, but alas, it's just me. No parents, no husband. It was easy for them to choose me. There's no one in this world who cares if I live or die." A small smile curves my lips. "Well, apart from you, it seems."

The merman leans forward in his chair. I could drown in the depth of his gaze. His fin-like ears twitch slightly.

"I do care."

The warmth inside me unfurls. It prickles along my arms and down my legs. Kindling hidden spots within me. The longer I stare at him, the clearer his handsome face becomes.

The sturdy bridge of his nose, the fullness of his lips. Heat covers me, the thin scrap of silk suddenly feels like it's smothering me. I rub my thighs together, trying to soothe the ache that's building there. None of this makes sense, and I suppose for now it doesn't have to.

I let myself feel and lose myself in his gaze. The merman is very handsome. Scales and all.

He leans closer, and my body mirrors him. I can scent saltwater on his skin. The pale strands of his hair shimmer like crystals. What would those scales feel like against my fingers? My lips? My pulse pounds, and his eyes dip to my neck as if he can hear it.

"Are you afraid of me?"

I raise a brow.

"Should I be?"

"No. No harm will ever come to you from me."

Biting my lip, I nod.

"I believe you," I say, shrugging. "Besides, what choice do I really have?"

"All of them," he responds quickly. "If you wish for me to leave you in peace, I will do so. Once you are healed, transportation will be arranged to take you anywhere you want to go. You have my word."

Shock momentarily steals my voice. He makes it sound so easy, but I guess it is for someone like him. He's not keeping me here. I'm free to go. I should accept his offer and never look back. So why am I hesitating?

"Or?"

He blinks. "Or?"

"Or," I repeat. "You made it sound like there was going to be a second option."

The merman grins, and my heart nearly pounds out of my chest. I bask in the warmth of his smile. I've never felt more alive.

"There is," he confirms.

"Good, because I don't want to be alone. Not right now."

Not ever, I think, but I manage to keep the words in. I've spent these last eight years floating through life without anchors. I belonged to no one and nothing. I watched the years of my life trickle by in unending days of loneliness. I had made peace with it—to live out my days in comfortable solitude.

That is still what I want.

However, I cannot deny the way the merman makes me feel. When he looks at me the way he is now, it's as if he sees me—truly sees me. The only one who's ever managed to glimpse my soul. It is fast, and it is sudden, but from the moment I awoke here, it felt like I've been suspended in a beautiful dream. One where anything is possible. One where I can let this fledgling desire inside of me run rampant.

I've stayed a virgin all these years mainly because I've never looked at another and wanted them the way I do this merman. In this dream, the possibility of learning what his body will feel like alongside mine doesn't seem out of reach. I can give myself to another wholeheartedly. The consequences of such action can't touch me here in my perfect dream.

Tonight, and only tonight, can be everything I've ever wanted. Tomorrow I can return to my safe, solitary life on land and keep the memories of my time under the waves with me forever.

That's the thing about dreams—even the most realistic ones—aren't meant to last.

"What do you want from me, Astryd? What can I give you?"

His words pull me from my thoughts. My decision is made. One night of reckless abandon, anymore than that would be unwise. I was a fool before, and I will not be so again.

"Your name for one."

The merman grins, sliding to his feet. Extending his hand, I lay mine against his massive palm. The feeling of his soft scales sliding against me makes goosebumps erupt on my flesh. He dips into a dramatic bow, his white hair flopping over his forehead.

"Qurill, my lady," he announces. "Prince of the Darksea."

His lips graze the back of my hand. Breath stills in my lungs as his eyes burn into mine. With some reluctance, he lets me go. I can feel the phantom press of his mouth as I settle my palm atop the silk.

"Qurill," I say, delighting in the way he shivers at my voice. "I cannot return to Bluewater. The villagers would just sacrifice me again. Besides, with the way things are, I don't have a job to go back to. If there was any way you could take me somewhere tomorrow—somewhere safe—I'd be grateful."

The merman—Qurill—nods, taking a few steps back from the bed.

"It will be done. I've bothered you for long enough. Surely you'd like some rest before our journey tomorrow."

Shaking my head, I slide off the bed. The cool title greets the naked soles of my feet. With both of us on the ground, my head barely grazes the center of his chest. My thighs are the size of his upper arms. My mouth goes dry as I crane my neck back to stare at him. Dampness spreads along my inner thighs.

"I've done enough resting." My hands grip the silk sheet to my chest. "I thought I was going to die today. I vowed to myself in those final moments that if I somehow made it out, I would live—truly live."

Qurill nods. I can feel his stare going through me, glimpsing into my soul. Whatever he finds there makes his eyes dance like blue flames.

"Will you help me do that? Give me today and show me things no other human has seen before I return to reality tomorrow."

As I spoke, our bodies drifted closer. His chest is barely an inch away from grazing my cheek. I breathe in his scent of seawater and the faint traces of sandalwood. I want to lick the salty droplets from his skin and feel his weight on top of me. My body prickles with awareness, beyond desperate to feel his touch.

My nipples press against the silk sheet. Liquid arousal streams down my thighs as I clench them together. The ache there is building into a crescendo I won't be able to ignore for much longer. Qurill's own breathing has turned ragged. His nostrils and gills flex with each deep inhale.

I would let him take me—on this bed or on the floor, it matters little. Whatever command he gave me, I would follow, if only to know what it meant to be close to another. Only he will do. I've never wanted someone this much, and I know in my heart I never will again. I want to celebrate being alive by giving myself over to the pleasures I've never experienced.

Tomorrow, I will return to the cautious woman who never takes risks, knowing it's safer to remain alone and unseen. Tonight is all I have to revel in my desires—to shed my fears and silence the mind that begs me to be careful.

This evening, with Qurill's help, I will be the one thing I've never been allowed: wild.

The Prince of the Darksea holds his palm out towards me, his eyes swirling like whirlpools.

"Come."

4

———

ASTRYD

Holding tightly to Qurill's hand, he carefully guides me along the cool tile floor of the palace.

His skin is warm against mine. His scent invades my lungs, tormenting my desire. Keeping the silk sheet tight to my chest with only one hand is a challenge. My bare feet have tangled in the fabric more times than I can count on the short journey we've made.

My breath catches once we reach the massive front doors. They are hewn from pale marble. Clam shells with glistening pearls are carved into their fronts. Golden handles rest above them, glimmering in the light. Qurill drops my hand, and I immediately itch for it back.

With a wave of his arm, the massive doors groan and peel back. Beyond the threshold is shimmering water. There seems to be an incandescent layer covering the surface of the water that ripples before my eyes. I turn towards the Prince of the Darksea and find that his gaze is already on mine.

My face warms under his intent stare.

"My magic keeps the sea out, but make no mistake, we are deep underwater." His eyes stray to my neck. "To keep you safe at these depths, I'll need to impart some of my magic on you as well."

Before I can ask what he means, something cool glides along my throat. Sandalwood fills my nostrils. I gasp as a sharp sting pierces my skin. My hands raise instinctively to the area. Instead of finding an injury, I find slick slivers of skin. They flutter against my fingers, the sensation unsettling and thrilling all at once.

"The gills will be temporary," Qurill confirms. "They will fully dry up once you return permanently to the surface."

"Is that what would happen to yours? If you stayed on land for too long?"

Qurill shakes his head.

"My mother is human—my father is of the sea. I am a child born to both worlds. I can exist fully in each without having to forsake my gills or human lungs."

I nod.

"That's handy."

Qurill chuckles softly before pressing his hand to my back. The soft touch of his palm against the silk sends prickles of awareness through my body. He urges me towards the open doors. My eyes widen as I take in the majesty before me.

Schools of colorful fish swim in synchronization, unaware of the small sharks close behind, navigating the water with their pointed noses. Seaweed floats by while coral and seagrass cover the jagged rocks of the ground below. The water is bright blue and barely looks real. Qurill must be awfully powerful to keep all this at bay.

As if in a trance, I lift my hand.

My finger pierces through the incandescent layer separating the palace from the sea. The water is cool and molds around my hand. I gasp as I pull my hand back, watching droplets of salt water fall to the tiles at my feet. I look up at

Qurill, who's watching me carefully, amusement dancing in his gaze.

My lips suddenly feel dry, and I snake my tongue out to lick them. Heat kindles in Qurill's gaze as he takes a step closer to me. Our bodies are nearly flush. My pulse pounds in response to his nearness.

"I thought we could explore some of my favorite coves. Swim with the fish and discover hidden places no human has ever seen before."

Qurill's voice is soft and rough all at once. Slowly, his hand lifts to my cheek, tracing along the smooth curve. My breath catches as his hand slowly lowers. Goosebumps erupt on my flesh as his fingers tease the top of the silk sheet still gripped in my hand.

He leans in. His lips find my ear, and my eyes flutter close.

"You might want to leave this behind," he whispers. "It'll tangle in the corral."

My cheeks warm at his words and his closeness. Biting my lip, I drop the sheet. Cool air caresses my naked skin. Qurill hisses beside me. I force my eyes open, refusing to feel shy. I've never been naked around a male before, but Qurill isn't any male. I'm giving myself to him today—I'm allowing myself to be reckless and selfish if only for tonight. There is no time to be timid.

I know what I want—I want him to see me. All of me.

Qurill steps back, I can feel his eyes looking over my body as if his stare was a physical caress. My pink nipples harden under his attention. I clench my thighs together, grateful we will soon both be wet, and I can hide the state of my arousal. His hand finds my chin and tips my eyes up towards him. He is so tall that my head tips all the way back in order for us to lock gazes.

"You are very beautiful, Astryd."

There's an edge to his voice. I let his compliment wash over me. To have spent so much of my life hidden, it feels ridiculously decadent to be on display like this. I nod my thanks as he drops his hand. We both turn towards the door at the same time.

"Do we just...dive right in?"

"Yes," Qurill says. "No time to delay."

He takes a step forward, and the reality of what we are doing catches up to me. Once again, I can't seem to stop being a fool. How had I not thought about this sooner?

"Wait." I grip his arm, turning towards him. "I—I'm not a very strong swimmer."

He raises a pale brow. "Meaning?"

Color floods my cheeks. "Meaning, I can float. As a means of survival, but swimming..."

I trail off, letting my sentence just linger there. Qurill's lips twitch as if he is fighting off a laugh. He walks behind me, leaning in close until his soft scales tease the skin of my back. A hardness presses against my backside, and I swallow a moan. Sweeping the hair off my neck, I feel his mouth at my ear once more.

"Don't worry, Astryd. I'll teach you." His hands trail down my arms before locking around my wrists. "Put your arms out in front of you. Fold your hands over each other and jump forward. I'll guide you through the next bit."

With a steadying breath, I do as he says. I leap forward with my hands extended. Crashing through the air bubble, cool water covers my skin. My gills flex along my neck, filtering the water so I can suck down lungfuls of air. I can keep my eyes open, no doubt another perk of his magic. Bubbles fly from my nose as my hands and feet slap around, trying and failing to tread water.

Large palms fall to my hips, holding me still. I turn, my hair flying around me in a dark gold veil. Qurill is beside me, amusement written in every line of his face.

"Relax," he says, though the words don't come from his mouth. They echo through my mind as if he speaks directly into my head.

"Can you hear me?" I ask in my mind.

"Yes."

"How?"

"Magic," he replies with a wry grin.

I'll have to be careful to keep my thoughts as innocent as possible. The last thing I need is for him to hear a thought before I'm ready to share it.

"I heard that too," he replies into my mind.

If the water weren't so cold, I'd surely be painted in scarlet. Keeping my mind carefully blank, I allow him to guide me through the water. Our slick bodies slide together as we part the water. Qurill frames me, lifting my hand to touch the floating seaweed. We pass through a school of fish, their colors dazzling up close.

They swim between us, skimming my bare legs as they pass by. Once we are in open water, Qurill releases me, and panic begins to set in.

"Remain calm, Astryd. Panicking is the worst thing you can do."

He floats beside me, indicating I should mimic his body. Once I am certain I'm not going to float away, he kicks his feet slowly below him. I follow his movements. He begins pumping his arms, and I do the same. It's not long before I'm treading water with more success than I previously had.

"Very good, Astryd." His praise washes over me as I continue to tread water. "Now, turn to your side and repeat the motions. I'll be right beside you."

I do as he says, relishing in how easy it is to follow his commands. Floating onto my side, I kick my feet and move my arms in a similar fashion. I'm sailing through the water in no time. I spin and dive deeper. My hands trail over the bumpy texture of the coral and weave through the long strands of the seagrass. Pushing off from the jagged edge, I swim up from the floor and return to Qurill.

"You're a natural."

I smile at his words, floating near him and hooking my hand around his.

"I have a good teacher."

We carry on through the water together. Hours must pass as we explore hidden underwater coves, illuminated by glowing algae. Qurill takes me deeper into the sea, showing me a large shipwrecked vessel, broken along the seafloor. Inside, we pilfer through the treasure eaten away by the marine life. Qurill guides me from the ship and allows us to be swallowed up by a large school of fish. They wrap us in a cocoon of shimmering bodies.

Qurill and I press close, my nipples digging into his chest. His hands fall to my waist, holding me tightly to him. We stare up at each other. Our mouths are close enough to touch. My heart pounds against my ribs as his hands trail lower. He stares at me, his blue eyes begging for permission. I give it with a slight nod.

His fingers press into the globes of my ass. My head falls forward against his chest. This is reckless, and even if I had vowed to myself to let it happen, there is still a voice telling me to stop. Even knowing that we will part tomorrow, and as much as I will treasure this time together, taking this next step will make it harder to walk away from him.

Yet, I must. He's given me no promises of forever—not that I've given him any indication that I would like such a vow.

I'm getting ahead of myself. He is offering me exactly what I want: a night to feel alive again. Besides, isn't it better to end this now before I get too attached? If I did decide to stay, the pain would be worse when he eventually turned to another for comfort and discarded me. I'm ruining the gift

I've been given. I will not let that small voice dictate my choices tonight.

Perhaps that's why this all feels so right. Our time together is limited—the frenzied need to have him is spurned by knowing we will part come morning. I can tell he feels the same, at least for tonight. I can feel his arousal—see the way his eyes heat when he looks at my naked skin. He called me beautiful and has shown me his most cherished hidden spots. That has to mean something.

There is another small voice—one much more dangerous than the one telling me to be cautious—that is brewing in my heart. I don't know the last time I've enjoyed myself like this. Or the last time I've been so cared for. For a moment, as I gaze up into his eyes, I allow myself to succumb to the fantasy of what being with him would be like. Spending the days in bed with my savior, trusting him to take care of all my needs, and never returning to my lonely life on the surface.

We could share a life of magic and pleasure inside his palace. We would spend hours exploring the vast sea, then wringing ourselves out with pleasure every evening.

It is a beautiful fantasy, one that cannot be.

Scissoring my thighs in the water, I am desperate for relief. Qurill's muscles tighten against me, and I look up. Blue flames burn me alive as his hold on me strengthens. My face heats, and I pray he did not hear my conflicting thoughts.

Qurill's face remains peaceful as he releases his hold on my ass. His hands skim up my side before taking my hand in his once more.

"Come." He swims us out from the school of fish. "My favorite cove is just over here."

I keep a tight hold on him as we glide through the water. The curved opening of the cove nears. Once inside, I see that the interior is only partially submerged. A rocky ledge extends from the stone wall. Glowing algae prowls along the walls, casting everything in a bluish light. With his help, Qurill carefully lifts me onto the ledge.

I gasp as I break through the water's surface. My mouth opens as I adjust to breathing normally again. Water pours down my body. The moss and algae cushion my back as I lie panting.

Qurill emerges from the watery depths below. He hoists himself onto the rock beside me, his legs still dangling in the water. Salt water slides down his body, droplets collecting in the deep cuts of his muscles. I itch to lick the water collected there. A damp breeze permeates the cove. I shiver from the air but also at Qurill's intense gaze.

I suddenly realize just how naked I am. My hair is plastered to my breasts. I inch my thighs together and sit up slowly. Qurill's pupils expand, nearly devouring his blue irises. His chest rises and falls rapidly before he shakes himself and looks away.

"We should get back." It's jarring to hear his voice outside of my mind. "You must be hungry."

As if in response, my stomach rumbles loudly. With a sharp nod, Qurill braces his impressive forearms on the rocky ledge in preparation for diving back into the water. I move before I realize I'm doing so. My hand goes to his wrist, stopping him.

There's no going back. If I'm being honest, this was always going to happen. I want him too much—it's sudden and reckless, but it doesn't change the fact of how much I need him right now.

I'll deal with the consequences of my broken heart tomorrow when I'm alone again.

"What if," I pause, licking my lip. "What if I'm hungry for more than just food?"

Qurill groans, his whole body tightening. He turns towards me, looming over my body. Power radiates from him. Strong fingers dig into the algae along the stone.

"What are you asking me for, Astryd?"

I meet his gaze, my decision kindling inside me like an inferno.

"I want you to show me more than just the sea. Show me everything, please."

Qurill's body jerks. His eyes devour me.

"Everything," he growls. "Pleasure?"

I nod frantically, sweat breaking out along my skin.

"Tonight I can be free—tomorrow you'll take me ashore and all of this will feel like a distant dream," I say in a rush. "I'll return to my comfortable solidarity, and I want to have a piece of today—of you—with me when I do. I almost died today. I want to be reminded that I am very much alive."

Qurill looms closer. His body is nearly directly over mine.

"What would you like me to do to you, Astryd?"

Biting my lip, I shrug.

"Don't feel like I'm pressuring you. This is a bold demand. If you do not wish to—"

"However you want me," Qurill purrs, his hand wrapping gently around my ankle, "I will gladly oblige all your desires."

His fingers skim along my ankle bone. I gasp as my thighs slide apart on their own accord. I'm baring myself to his gaze. Qurill groans, using his hand to slide my one foot even further along the rock. My stomach quivers in anticipation.

"Maybe we could—well, I'm not sure." I sound breathless. "Perhaps, we should kiss?"

It sounds more like a question than a demand. I want to kick myself. Qurill chuckles darkly, shaking his head from side to side. Damp hair curls along his fin-like ears as he shifts between my thighs.

"A kiss on the mouth is so trivial." There is a wicked gleam in his eyes. "Let me bestow one on your pretty cunt. That will make you feel alive."

My breath catches as both his hands hook around my

ankles. He slides them apart, settling them as far as they will go. My inner thighs burn slightly, but any ache is forgotten as he lowers his face to my core. His warm breath tickles my damp flesh. I feel no nerves about him seeing me like this. I want him so badly I feel like I may perish at any moment.

Licking his blue lip, his eyes meet mine. Red decorates my knees and chest.

"Has any man ever touched you here? Seen you like this?"

I shake my head. Words are beyond me. Qurill grins, hooking his hands under my knees and tossing them over his massive shoulders.

"Good," he purrs. "One less murder I have to commit tomorrow."

Before I can respond, the broad side of his tongue skims up my slit. I scream at the wet glide of his muscle against me. He presses his mouth to me, his nose inhaling deeply against the patch of golden hair covering my feminine flesh.

"Tonight, I will be your master," he whispers onto my damp skin. "The one who gives you unimaginable pleasure—the one whose memory no human man could ever fuck out of you."

"Qurill," I pant. "Please."

"You want to test my vow, Astryd? Let me show you the pleasures that await you in my bed."

With a snarl, he devours me fully. He licks my pussy from top to bottom. His tongue slithers inside of me, pumping deeply. His fingers dig into my hips, raising me against his face. I canter my hips, rubbing my clit against his nose, greedy for all the friction I can get. My hands fall to his head, the soft strands of hair shifting through my fingers.

His mouth makes sloppy wet sounds as he pleasures me. His lip latches onto my clit as my back bows off the rock. He releases me with a pop. My vision is beginning to blur. An unknown peak looms before me, and I long to be tossed off it.

"Give me your eyes, Astryd," Qurill commands. "I want to see just how much you can take."

My jaw goes slack as I watch him suck two fingers into his mouth. With trembling thighs, my anticipation grows as he glides his slick digits through my folds.

"You're so wet—you hardly need this."

He spits down onto my pussy, causing me to moan. His foamy saliva lands on my clit and slides down my slit until it collects at my entrance. His index finger swirls around my opening. My breath catches at the sensation of being filled for the first time. His insertion is slow, and his tongue licks my clit the entire time he invades me.

His name falls from my lips.

"Tight little pussy. I can't wait to feel you stretch around my cock."

I nod frantically. This is good, but I want more. I want everything. My body is alive. I'm merely a vessel for him to pleasure. I am for him to use however he sees fit because I know he will give me the completion I desire.

"Please."

"Soon," he vows. "Let me make you come first."

He pulls his finger back before adding another. My heart pounds as he scissors them inside me. He's careful not to go too deep. His rough pumps inside me make my head spin. My thighs begin to squeeze his head as pleasure pounds through me.

Withdrawing his fingers from me, his hand slaps down sharply on my clit. I scream, pleasure dancing on every nerve ending. The bite of pain enhances my desire. Qurill smiles as if he knew I'd like it. He seems to know my body better than I do.

"Tonight, I own every inch of you. Your sopping wet cunt—"

He tips my hips up further. Qurill's finger, slick with my arousal and his saliva, presses against my back entrance. He slides into me slowly, laying claim to all I am.

"And your tight asshole." He presses a kiss to my clit as his finger sheaths fully into my backside. "Come on my face while I fuck your ass with my finger. Now."

His tongue spears into me, reaching as deep as it can. I scream as both his finger and tongue work me in tandem. I can feel both gliding against each other inside me. My chest rises and falls as my skin glistens with sweat. The air around us is damp. The scent of salt and our coupling mingle into a heady combination.

I've never felt anything like this. Pleasuring myself with my own hand has never yielded such intense results. When my peak comes, I may die at the sheer force of it. I've been moved past the point of pleasure. I am just an object to be used for his desire—and I've never been happier. I want to be completely owned by him.

When his other hand begins rubbing tight circles on my clit, I erupt.

"Qurill!" I scream as pleasure washes over me.

My whole body locks down. My ass clenches around his finger while my pussy strangles his tongue. The world around me blurs as each muscle in my body strains. Fire churns in my belly, filtering out into my fingers and toes. Wave after wave crashes over me, threatening to drown me in its pleasurable depth.

Qurill continues to lick me, even once my muscles give out and I fall limply to the rock. My body shakes with aftershocks as he pulls his finger from my ass. He licks me clean before pressing a final kiss to my clit.

His eyes are completely black as he prowls up my body. Seawater drops onto my naked skin as he looms over me. I open my arms and eagerly accept his weight. His mouth falls onto mine, sealing the pleasure he just gave me with our first kiss. I'm not nearly as practiced as him but it feels right all the same. Just like he taught me to swim, his tongue teaches mine to glide with his.

I taste my arousal, and I moan. My hands hook around his head, holding him firmly against me. His hand falls to my breasts, roughly shaping my aching nipples in his palm. I groan against his mouth until we finally break for air. He kisses along my jaw, tracing along my skin as he reaches my ear.

"Your town sacrificed you to my father," he whispers, "but it is I who will lay claim to you tonight."

Qurill thrusts his hardness against me. I whimper at the size of the bulge straining against his leather pants. My mouth waters, and my satiated body is now aching for even more pleasure.

"I will possess you so deeply, no human man will ever satisfy you."

The words are growled possessively against my ear. The thought of me with another is abhorrent to us both. He squeezes my breast tightly, marking me with his fingertips.

"When I leave tomorrow, you'll return to the sea every night naked—calling out for me to fuck you amongst the waves or atop the sandy shore. Wherever I want, whenever I want."

"Qurill," I sigh, turning my head for another kiss.

He obliges. His mouth devastates mine. The vows he's just given make my heart ache. I know he is right. It will be nearly impossible for me to leave him tomorrow, but I will. The only thing I can do now is leave a part of me behind so that my memory will torment him just as his torments me.

"Let's get you fed," he declares, breaking our kiss. "You'll need your strength to endure our night together."

I nod eagerly, wrapping my arms around his neck. He tucks my body into his chest and plunges us back into the water. Holding on to him tightly, he navigates us through the sea until the palace looms ahead. The small voice inside me telling me to be wary is silent for once as we approach the towering structure.

Caution be damned, life is meant to be lived. At least for tonight.

QURILL

Astryd clings to me as we cut through the water. The way she tightly holds me makes me glow with pleasure. She is everything I have ever wanted—beautiful, adventurous, and adrift, just like me. I want to show her she'll never be alone again. That she can find safe harbor in my port. Forever, if she'd allow it. I'll take care of everything if she agrees to be mine. It would be my privilege to care for her. It is the role I was born to fulfill.

I hadn't meant to hear her private thoughts. The magic that lets us communicate is fickle, and while I had tried to be noble and not pry, she was too great a temptation. I want to know everything about her—her likes and dislikes. What makes her happy, how to satisfy her properly so that she may never wish to leave my side.

Because, despite everything, she does still wish to leave. There is a conflict raging inside of her. One forged from the necessity of self-preservation. I understand why she is wary of someone like me. She has been alone for so long with no one looking out for her. To throw away a simple life of solitary security in favor of running off with a merman you just met seems a bit foolish.

Even if being together feels as natural as breathing. I would spend every moment together, reaffirming that she had not made a mistake in trusting me.

I want to keep her—more than I've ever wanted anything in my life. She is mine, and she is giving me tonight to prove it. I have until dawn for her to change her mind and realize her place is at my side and in our bed. The moment she dove into the sea, fearless and naked, her fate was sealed to mine. It is sudden, but just because it is fast doesn't make it any less real.

Astryd fears I will grow bored with her, but there is no chance of that. She will satisfy me for the rest of my days as I will her. I will prove to her that we deserve more time. Even if it is not forever, she wants to give me, I would eagerly take another day, a week, a month—whatever more I could get before she returns to the surface.

I feel her slipping away already. Even as she holds tightly to me, there is a part of her that has already begun to slip away. I must grab hold of her while I still can.

She is my future, even if I am not hers. The way my father described meeting my mother makes more sense to me now than ever. It is an instant and overwhelming feeling when you find the other half of your soul. It consumes and unsettles you. This primal need to stake my claim on her fully pounds through my veins.

That is why I will not give in to despair. I will follow her forever, hoping she'll change her mind if she does wish to return to the surface tomorrow. There is still time to win her over—I cannot lose my mate when I have only just found her.

Our naked skin slides together as we pass through other schools of rainbow fish. Her hand extends to graze their scaly bodies. She gasps, her blue eyes taking in her surroundings. If she thinks these wonders are marvelous, I'll show her every hidden wonder the sea has to offer. Today was a drop in the bucket compared to what the world has to offer.

There would be nothing off-limits to her. I will indulge and satisfy her curiosity. She will be well cared and provided for.

And loved most of all.

Had she not felt that between us earlier? The way she called out to me as I feasted on her cunt solidified our bond. I can still taste her sweetness along my tongue. She was hot and wet, delirious in her need for me and me alone. Her heart had reached for mine. I felt it.

Perhaps to her, this feels like only lust. A need to satisfy a longstanding ache. If it is, that desire can be stoked into something more permanent. She wants me the way I am—in my true form. I've never laid with anyone looking like this. Astryd is not repulsed by me. There is only desire and longing in her gaze as she beheld my naked torso.

Could it not be clearer that we were meant for each other?

I will make good on my vow. The pleasure I am about to unleash on her body no mortal man can compete with. If she chooses to leave, she will wade through the seawater, calling out for me, knowing no one will ever satisfy her as thoroughly as I can. She'll beg me to fuck her, and I will oblige until she finally gives in and lets me keep her beneath the waves.

The palace comes into view. The pocket holding the seawater back parts for us easily. We splash onto the tile floor. I cushion her body against mine as I watch her suck down lungfuls of air. Water slides down her body, and her hair drips on my chest.

She smiles up at me, even as she begins to shiver. Quickly, I set her on her feet and go in search of fresh towels. Once located, I wrap one around her body and use another to blot dry her hair. She relaxes against me as I tend to her wet strands. When I am satisfied with how dry her hair is, I toss the towel aside and prowl in front of her.

Her eyes sparkle up at me. Color dances beneath the freckles on her cheeks. I trace her soft skin with my thumb, loving how she leans into me.

"Are you still sure you want me to take you?" I ask.

Biting her lip, Astryd nods softly. The flush on her face travels down to her chest. Her sweetness hangs heavy in the air. I long to savor her arousal directly from the source again.

"It feels right for it to be you," she confesses. "I've never wanted another like this."

Satisfaction unfurls in my chest. I cup her cheek, tipping her head even farther back so that she can see the need in my eyes. I want her for more than just a night of pleasure. I need her by my side. I need to keep her safe.

"Then you shall have me. All of me."

Her smile turns sad.

"Only for tonight," she adds. "I want to give this part of me to you. To remember me by."

"You can stay longer." I hear the desperation in my voice. "However long you want."

Astryd blinks rapidly before looking away. Her sadness is palpable. Back inside the palace, her mind is shut off to me, but I know her well enough to see the thoughts swirling in her mind. She has made her decision, but I'll be damned if I don't try to persuade her otherwise.

However, I don't want to push her away. I have to bide my time. I promised her pleasure, and I intend to deliver. My thumb drifts to her bottom lip as I pull her gaze back towards mine.

"Let's not talk about the future," I sigh. "Not when the present is so much sweeter."

Heat kindles in her gaze. Her naked body is flushed. I long to strip the towel off her and glimpse the supple curves beneath. In fact, that's what I'll do at this very moment.

The heavy fabric hits the tile with a thud. She gasps as

goosebumps erupt on her flesh. She is all pillowy softness. Golden skin glimmers in the low evening light. Her breasts are full, and her hips are round. Shapely thighs hide the hidden treasure between them that's already dripping. Pink nipples stand at attention, begging for my mouth.

I gently thumb one, loving how her head falls back.

"I must apologize to you. It seems I've been remiss in not giving you a proper kiss."

The ones after I feasted on her cunt were sweet, but I want my kiss to devastate her. I want it to set her on edge, so by the time I graze her pussy she's coming at the first slight touch. Her lips part as her eyes flutter closed. My lips swipe over hers. She's so soft—ripe for the taking.

Without warning, I bend down and throw her over my shoulder. She laughs as she hangs down my back. My arm holds her tightly under her knees. One hand smacks her ass, delighting in the pink that blooms on her soft skin. She moans, her arousal deepening. I walk quickly to our bedroom. I deposit her on the bed, her rosy cheeks pulled tight as she grins up at me.

This is the room I first brought her to after rescuing her. The primary suite is meant to house a king. This will be our royal bedchamber. I'll learn every inch of her body in the room, starting tonight.

Her mouth parts, and she makes quite the picture on our bed. Legs spread to reveal her glistening pussy. Her breasts rise and fall. Astryd's full, pink mouth gives me a wicked idea. One I need her standing for.

I pull her from the bed and into my arms. My fingers shift through her damp hair and hold her firm. Our mouths meet with a mutual groan. My tongue licks over her lips, which she eagerly parts. The dance of our tongues makes my knees buckle. She moans into my mouth.

The taste of sweet sunshine coats my tongue.

Her blunt nails rake down my back. My hand drifts between us to palm her breast. It fills my hand completely. There are a million different things I want to do to them. Lick them, bite them, fuck them. I want to paint them in my seed and watch her lick it off.

My mind spins as I kiss her harder. If she is to return to the surface tomorrow, she will go bearing my marks and with my seed in her pretty cunt. My cock rages between us. Astryd groans as she shifts between us, rubbing herself against my aching hardness. Seed already drips from the tip, strengthening my decision.

I break our kiss, watching her blue eyes blink open as she sucks down air. I smooth her swollen lips with my thumb.

"Will you let me have complete control over you tonight? Submit to me fully?"

Astryd shivers, her eyes glazing over. I can see her need to be controlled by a worthy male. She's had to shoulder so much responsibility for so long. She wants to hand over those burdens—her choices to me. I will guard her submission with my life. It is a privilege to be given this control over her. I will ensure she never regrets doing so.

Her golden hair floats down her back. She glows like a goddess as her hands reach out and wrap around my neck. Her body presses against mine as she sighs.

"Yes," she says, her mouth finding mine again.

Her promise washes over me. My blood burns hot in my veins. I drop her breast in favor of cupping her ass and dragging her against me. She rubs her body against me, trying to get some relief for herself. I work her against my front, my tongue moving in her mouth. It mimics the way my cock is going to fuck her later.

Once she is breathless, I pull back. Her eyes fall to my hands as I go to the waistband of my pants. I quickly undo the ties and push them down. I kick away the offending fabric and hear her intake of breath as she stares at my cock. Glistening seed makes the tip gleam.

Astryd licks her lips as I roughly smear the seed along my length. Perfect, she is absolutely perfect. With one rough pump, I could come just from looking at her.

She breathes heavily as I reach behind her and grab a large pillow. I toss it onto the floor between us. Astryd looks up at me from under her lashes, color staining her face and chest. My fingers trace along her jaw before cupping her shoulder.

"Get on your knees," I command, pushing down on her softly.

Her breath hitches. Black pupils expand as her pulse pounds at her throat. She shivers, hesitating at my command. That will not do.

"Astryd." My tone is stern, making her eyes jerk up to mine. "Do you wish to be punished?"

Her breathing becomes more ragged as she quickly blinks. Shaking her head, I press down on her shoulder again.

"Then do as you're told."

Swallowing thickly, I watch her spine straighten. Slowly, she lowers herself to her knees, cushioned by the large pillow. Pleasure floods my veins. Astryd is on her knees before me, looking gorgeous and submissive. She is mine to do with as I please. I own her. Tonight.

Forever.

Fisting my cock again, I approach slowly. The leaking tip is level with her lips. She stares up at me, beautiful and trusting. My seed boils, needing to be released onto her smooth skin and to fill her to the brim. I've never felt this way about another. In the past, I've always been a dominant lover, but I haven't needed the control as I do with Astryd.

She belongs to me, and I intend to enjoy her fully.

"I thought you might want to get better acquainted with my

cock," I offer, swiping the tip against her lips. "It's going to be spending a great deal of time inside you."

Astryd nods, tentatively taking me into her small hand. She smells like sunshine and fresh flowers. Her arousal makes my mouth water as she slowly drags her fist up and down my length. She cannot wrap her hand entirely around it. Her innocent eyes stare up at me, looking for praise and inflaming my desire.

"Good girl," I growl. "Grip me harder."

She does as I say. Her fist glides along my length with rough strokes. Pleasure pounds at the base of my spine as I watch her work me. Arousal glistens on her thighs. She rubs them together, clearly enjoying this as much as I am.

"Open your mouth, Astryd. Taste me."

Sucking in breath, she does as I command. She is the most obedient lover who will be rewarded for her efforts.

Her pink tongue sneaks out and carefully licks the head of my cock. A fresh spurt of my seed lands on her tongue. Moaning, she swallows it down, staring up at me. I'm transfixed as I watch her lick along my head and shaft. Her hand continues to work me as her tongue traces the soft scales covering my cock. Soft lips glide along my length as her hand teases the underside of my cock.

"Am I doing good?" she whispers. "Am I pleasing you?"

Her soft voice nearly sends me to my knees. I nod frantically, shuffling my fingers through her hair.

"You're perfect. Take me into your mouth—down your pretty throat."

She hiccups in surprise before nodding. Her jaw unhinges as she slides the head of my cock into her mouth. The wet glides of her tongue over my cockhead set my body on fire. She moans as she sucks me, her fist meeting her mouth as her head bobs along my length. Saliva pours at the corners of her mouth. It coats her chin and slides down her throat.

Still, she works me deep. Even as I bump the back of her throat and she chokes, she merely coughs on my length before retreating fully. Tears burn in her blue eyes, but I'm given no reprieve as she takes me deep again. The wet cavern of her mouth is a delight. I shift my hips and slide forward on her tongue. Her nose bumps against my stomach as she chokes once more. I grip her head and hold her in place.

Once satisfied, I release her and slide out of her throat. Coughing and sputtering, she blinks up at me. She's never looked more beautiful than she does right now. Tear-stained and with my cock in her mouth, I'll tuck this image into my heart in case I never get to experience such pleasure again.

"You're doing so well."

She preens under my praise, licking the side of my cock. Once more, she begins to fuck me deep, her tongue caressing the underside of my shaft.

"Give me some teeth, and I'll reward you with my seed," I inform her. "The first time I spill will be down your little throat. Isn't that what you want?"

"Yes," she garbles around my shaft.

Astryd works her neck back and forth on my length. Her blunt teeth graze my soft scales. Black dots erupt in my vision.

"You suck my cock like you were born to do it. Work for my seed. Earn it."

My fingers tighten in her hair as she nods frantically. I watch her hand slip between her thighs, rubbing tight circles on her clit. I snarl, yanking on her hair with enough force to stop her movements.

"No touching your greedy pussy. Only I get to pleasure it."

Astryd groans, dropping her hand. I thrust my hips deep as her teeth slide along my shaft. Bumping the back of her throat, her tightness overwhelms me, and I let go. With a groan of her name, I release a torrent of seed down her throat. She chokes and gags, but swallows all that I give her. I drop her hair and push her shoulders back.

Aiming my cock, I coat her lips and chin with my seed. It drops in heavy globs onto her heaving chest. I use the head of my cock to spread my spend along her lips. She licks it up and stares up at me. I'm panting as she cups her breast and looks up at me. Wickedness dances in her gaze as she leans down and licks my come off her chest.

I've made a mess of her, and I love it. My vision slowly returns as I take in the sight of her. Swollen lips and covered in seed, she is perfect in every way.

"Astryd," I say hoarsely. "That was amazing."

Her shoulders shake as she smiles demurely.

"I wanted my reward."

Laughing, I pluck her from the bed and kiss her on the mouth. She moans against me. The taste of me on her tongue makes my head spin. I reach down and wipe at her skin with the pillow before discarding it. I toss her onto the bed, coming down between her slayed thighs.

"And you will be rewarded." My hand cups her dripping pussy. "Do you need release?"

She nods frantically, working herself against my palm in desperation.

"I'll need to get you nice and wet before you can take my cock." I spear two fingers inside her dripping sheath. Astryd moans as her head falls back onto the bed. "Looks like you're already halfway there."

I kiss down her body, stopping at each breast to give them adequate attention. I tease each of her nipples into hard points. Her hands fist the sheets at her side until her knuckles turn white. I pump her cunt again and again. Kissing down her stomach, I lick into her naval before continuing lower.

With my mouth hovering over her clit, I capture her eye and make her watch as I give her the ultimate pleasure. It only takes a few sucks of her clit for her to erupt. Arousal pours from her, soaking my thrusting fingers and palm. I finger-fuck her through her orgasm until she's shaking. Pulling my hand from her, I lick my fingers clean before my hands rest on either side of her head.

My cock bobs between us. I settle it on her stomach, and she gasps. It will be a lot, but my cock will bring her nothing but pleasure. She was built to take my pounding—I will lay claim to her tonight. Apprehension makes her jaw go slack as I feel her thighs begin to close.

I snarl, cupping her knee and shoving it away.

"Keep your fucking thighs open, Astryd. You want this. Tell me how badly."

She swallows, thrashing on the bed. I know she is afraid, but she has to learn to hand her fears over to me. I will not hurt her. Everything for her will be handled so long as she is mine. I want her trust more than anything. I need to hear her say it—to confirm what we both already know.

"I—I'm sorry. I want it—you," she sputters. "Please, Qurill. Please fuck me."

Her thighs fall wide open as her supplication is realized. My body shivers in satisfaction. She has given herself to me, and I will indulge us both tonight. Gripping my cock, I slap it against her clit, loving the way she keens for it. I glide the head through her wetness until it is slick with both our arousals. Tucking it just inside her entrance, I grit my teeth and push forward.

Her tight wetness surrounds me instantly. Astryd grips me like a vice. Her breath catches at my invasion. She holds completely still as I push forward slowly. My cock butts up against her virginity, and I spit out a curse. I lean down to capture her lips, urging her to submit with my tongue. She holds onto my straining forearms.

I push all the way into her, not stopping until I'm fully inside.

Swallowing her scream, I whisper words of adoration and encouragement to her. I hate that I've caused her pain—I never will again. The only discomfort she'll experience at my hand is the kind that will make her come even harder. I hold completely still as her body adjusts around me.

"Qurill," she whispers. "Please. I'm okay. More."

Her words are choppy, but I hear her plea. Retreating slightly, I push back inside her. My scales graze her inner walls until my head butts up against her womb. The thought of getting her pregnant is fleeting. I would love to have a child with her, but we need some time first. I don't want to share her with anyone right now—not even our child.

Besides, I'm not above much when it comes to claiming Astryd, but I would never bind her to me with a child. I'll just have to convince her to stay because of how badly she wants me.

I pull my hips back until only my cockhead is inside her. With a quick surge, I slam all the way back into her. She groans, her breasts jostling with the impact. I fuck her hard and deep, establishing a punishing rhythm.

Her hips lift to meet my thrusts. Lithe thighs wrap around my waist, holding me as close as possible. I kiss her mouth again, before trailing my lips to her ear.

"I don't know how I'm supposed to give you up," I whisper into her ear. "Knowing how snug and wet you are—how can I release this treasure between your legs back into the world? It needs to be kept and protected. Just as you do."

"Qurill," she groans.

"My desperate girl. Do you need to be fucked harder?"

"Yes!" she screams. "Yes, yes! Please."

I grin against her before pulling back. Taking her knees in my hands, I toss them over my shoulders. Holding her thighs tightly to my chest, I power into her from below. She is deliciously tight. Her hands cushion against my thighs that slap into her backside. She moans loudly, her mouth open with heavy sobs.

"You're so big," she whimpers. "I'm close."

My grin is pure satisfaction. I can feel her tightening down on me. One tweak of her clit and she'll come. She knows it too. I continue to fuck her over and over. Her pussy clenches down on me as her whole body goes tight. Holding her thighs to my chest, I fuck her over and over—and then stop.

I am frozen within her. The sound of our bodies slapping around the room dissipates. Astryd growls, sitting up straighter on the bed. I drop her legs and throw them apart. Her eyes are wide in shock as I chuckle darkly.

Shaking my head, I skim my hand along her quivering inner thigh.

"Did you really think I was going to let you off that easily?"

Astryd groans as I pull out of her. Quickly, I roll her onto her side and crawl up beside her. Smacking her ass, she jolts before settling back against me. I lift her top leg as I drag my cock through her wetness. My length glistens with her juices. Gripping it tightly, I press my head against her pink asshole.

Astryd thrashes her eyes, going wide as she stares at me over her shoulder.

"Did you really think I'd let you leave me, without laying claim to all your holes?" I tsk slightly shaking my head. "Surely you should know me better than that."

"Qurill, please. I—I don't think—"

My lips kiss her temple, nuzzling into her before finding her ear again.

"Don't worry, Astryd. I'll fuck your ass next time."

I don't give her a chance to respond—a chance to say that this is the only time we can be together. Without another word, I plunge my cock deep into her pussy. Astryd screams as she claws at the sheets. I hold her hip as I fuck into her ruthlessly.

My hips bounce off her ass. Her hand reaches behind me to tangle in my hair and hold my face to her.

Cupping her jaw, I let my mask slip and allow my primal nature to take charge. Her pussy tightens on my hammering cock. We both need this. We need each other.

"You were made for this, Astryd. Made to be my little fuck-toy," I snarl. "I'll leave you ruined on the surface. How long do you think you'll last without this? A day? A week?" She groans, shaking her head as I continue. "When you need me again, just walk naked into the sea. I'll find you and give you my cock. I promise."

"Qurill," she moans. "Please. I'm close—let me come. Please."

I'm not surprised she doesn't say anything to my declaration. I can still make her come. Once she does, she'll see why she can't leave me. No other male will be worthy of her submission. She needs me to look out for her. She'll see that soon enough.

I continue to thrust into her roughly before snaking my hand around to the front of our bodies. Finding her clit, I work tight circles on it. Astryd gasps, her whole body locking down. Her eyes are wide and unseeing—a scream sticks in her throat. She clamps down on me like a fist as she comes.

I thrust deep one more time, my teeth biting into her shoulder as I pump deep and empty myself. Her greedy pussy drinks down my seed. It spills inside her in a rush. There is so much of it, it squelches between us, staining the silk sheets below. I stay inside her until her shocks of pleasure subside. Gently pulling out, another fresh rush of seed coats her inner thighs.

Turning her in my arms, I hold her close. She nuzzles under my chin. I feel her heart pounding against mine. I can feel our souls weaving together. She is my mate, and while she is human, she has to feel it too. We are meant to be together. In the bliss after our coupling, I've never been more certain of anything in my life.

I kiss her sweaty brow. She blinks up at me, tipping her chin so that I can taste her lips. Our kiss is chaste. The gentleness of it makes my heart pound. I touch our foreheads together and stare into her blue eyes.

"Are you alright?"

She smiles up at me, tucking a piece of my hair behind my ear. Her fingers trace my fin, causing me to shiver.

"I'm wonderful."

Staring at her is like glimpsing into the future. I can picture us like this every morning and night. Spending our days exploring and spending our evenings marking each other inside and out. Even though I was buried inside her less than a minute ago, I can already feel her slipping away. Our time together is shortening with every second.

The comforting silence of our coupling begins to turn cold. Panic sets in. She has not changed her mind, I can see that on her face. I've shown her the pleasure I can give her—that she would be safe with me and well taken care of, and yet it is not enough. She still wants to leave me. I can't let that happen, and I am not above begging.

"Don't go," I whisper. "Remain here with me as long as you like, but please, don't let this end tonight. Please, Astryd."

Her hand drifts to my cheek, gently thumbing my cheekbone. Her smile is small and sad. Red rims her eyes as she blinks away the gathering moisture.

"I cannot stay, Qurill."

Her words are soft and final.

Hopelessness is an anchor around his ankle, dragging him down into the murky depths. I want to argue with her, to fuck her again, and remind her who's mastered her body. I want to lay bare my own soul and tell her how much I love her. That would be cruel to do so. Not to mention unwise. I wouldn't want her to stay with me out of pity.

Astryd's soft lips press against mine.

"Just let me have tonight. Please."

I nod, unsure what to say next. I failed. I did not prove myself to her, and now I'm going to lose her. Not completely, even when I leave her on the surface, I'll keep watch over her for the rest of her life. I'll be her shadow—the figure in the distance that always seems to be following her. I couldn't stop myself even if I tried.

Astryd's stomach growls to life between us. Even though I loathe having to leave her, I'm grateful for the task of providing for her.

"Let me get you something to eat."

I leave the room and collect a steaming plate of fish and seasoned rice. Returning to the bed, Astryd has slid beneath the ruined sheets. She says nothing as I hand the plate over towards her. The easy quiet we once shared has disintegrated. Her mind is made up. Any attempt to sway her decision will just push her further away. I watch her eat from the corner of the bed.

She picks at her food for a few moments before setting the plate aside. Settling under the sheets, her hair fans out on the pillow. Her body is tense, and I hate that. Still, I don't want to waste a moment of her being here.

I crawl up behind her and lay my arm against her waist. Immediately, she relaxes, settling against me. I kiss her soft shoulder and breathe in her sweet scent, committing it to memory. Her breathing soon deepens and becomes even. Staring down at her beautiful face, I can see her adventurous spirit hovering beneath the surface. It longs to be freed but has been caged by years of self-preservation.

My only hope now is that she'll do as I said and reach out to me when she needs to be pleasured. It's the only hope I have to hold onto. If I return her to the surface and keep my distance, perhaps I'll give her a chance to miss me.

I spend the next few hours cataloging all the freckles on her shoulders.

Dawn is only a few hours away, and though I hate to leave her with so little time remaining, there is still a wrong that needs to be righted. The man who chained her will soon find himself in a watery grave. I'll enjoy this kill—knowing it'll keep Astryd safe.

I'll be her protector—her shadow. Even if she doesn't want me to be.

6

ASTRYD

The small rowboat bobs along each gentle wave.

The morning sun has fully risen, casting the barren sandy beach ahead in soft shadows. Atop the hill, I can make out the thatch roofs of town. It looks very similar to Bluewater. However, we are far enough away that no one from my old village will discover me.

Qurill silently rows the small vessel towards our destination. Neither one of us speaks. The only sound comes from the seagulls calling above.

This morning had been a sullen affair. I had awoken with Qurill beside me. His deep breathing had nearly lulled me back to sleep. I couldn't delay the inevitable, so there in the dark, I categorized everything about him. His scales, his scent, the sharp angles of his face. I memorized every detail before waking him up, asking to be returned to the surface.

We hadn't spoken more than that. There are many things we aren't saying to each other. It would be unwise for me to share what was really in my heart—especially as I've resolutely told him that I can't stay.

Even though I want to, more than anything—even though I love him.

I love Qurill. I know it to be true. Yesterday was the best day of my life, and without him, I shall never experience it again. We were one in his bed. Our hearts and souls had fused together, forging us on a new path. One where we would always be by each other's side. At least, that was the case on my side.

My heart is begging me to stay—to tell him that I've made a mistake. However, my mind tells me this is the right move. I should return to the surface and live amongst humans like me. I could tell him I love him, and maybe for a time, he would be happy. But he is immortal, wouldn't he eventually grow bored with me? Our passion was surely not common, yet could it keep a creature like him satisfied forever?

Those doubts keep me from confessing my true feelings.

I've tried all morning to make peace with this decision. Realistically, it is my best option. I can start over in a new town, rebuild my savings, and live the quiet, comfortable life of solitude I've been working towards. My future never included another. I hadn't dreamed of a husband or children of my own —my parents' deaths devastated me enough to want to spare my child the same position I was in. It is safer to be alone; no one can leave me or grow bored with our time together.

So while I'm giving up on my happiness, I'll have my freedom, and that's something most young women can't say.

I'll tuck the memory of my time with Qurill into my heart. I've had adventures thanks to him. The need for anymore is a childish fantasy. While Qurill commanded my body and my heart, he didn't make any vows before telling me I could stay longer. He clearly got pleasure from our coupling, as did I. But was that all it was to him?

He didn't say he loved me. I could be his lover for a time, but eventually I would return to the surface like I am now. Only to be a shell of myself, grieving a heart broken by time. At least now, we are parting on amicable terms. It is my decision to leave—at least that's what I tell myself.

Before I realize it, the boat runs ashore. Wet sand piles up along the smooth sides of the hull. Qurill exits first, and I watch as his muscles bunch and tighten. He holds a hand out to me. Not meeting his gaze, I take it.

He settles me down on the sand. The damp ground soaks my new silk slippers. The hem of my green dress clings to my ankles. I am a touch tender between my thighs. I savor the ache, willing it never to leave me. The memory of him is fresh, and I don't want time to dull it.

I swallow thickly, finely brave enough to look up into his eyes. Blue fire sparkles down at me. He is guarded in a way I haven't seen before.

How long will it be until he forgets me? It was a magical night for me, but he will certainly invite another human into his bed. Will I be lost in his sea of lovers? My heart aches at the thought of our night not meaning as much to him as it did to me.

I'll never forget him—not as long as I live.

Qurill breaks our stare to nod upwards. The beach slopes up between two rocky cliffs. The faint hum of voices trickles down the hill.

"The town of Watership is just up there. There will be plenty of housing and job options for you."

I nod, the salty breeze blowing strands of my blonde hair into my eyes. Qurill opens his mouth as if to say more, but merely shakes his head. He reaches into his pocket, pulling out a small cloth bag. He hands it towards me, and I take it, marveling at the impressive weight for such a small item.

Licking my lips, I can hear my heart pounding as I untie the strings. The sight inside steals my breath. Dozens of golden coins and sparkling jewels of all colors gleam up at me. Glimmering pearls roll around amongst the treasures.

"Qurill," I breathe.

This is too much. I cannot accept this. I—

Qurill closes my hand around the bag. I savor his touch, memorizing the weight and feel of his hands. My heart screams at me that I'm making a mistake. Why can't I be brave enough to let go of my pride—of my doubts—and claim what I really want?

"Take it, Astryd. Please." His grip on me tightens. "Let me take care of you in some small way. I need you somewhere safe —living comfortably."

His earnest gaze decides me. I nod. At my agreement, he releases my hand. One of his fingers curls around a stray blonde lock of hair. He rubs it between his thumb and forefinger. Tucking it behind my ear, I shiver as he skims over the shell of my ear. His hand travels lower—a feather-like touch—before cupping my cheek.

"Yesterday was the most extraordinary day of my life. I shall treasure it and you always."

My breath catches on a sob. Tears burn my eyes, but I refuse to let them fall. Where is my voice? I should confess my love to him. Better to have loved and lost than to never have loved at all, isn't that what people say? I have no idea. My mind is a jumbled mess. I can't make sense of the warring thoughts within me.

The only thing that I can think to do is tilt my head back and welcome his soft lips on mine. Our kiss is bruising. He groans against me, and I eagerly part my mouth. His tongue sweeps inside, laying claim to me one final time. I surrender to him and this moment. He takes my mouth roughly, and I love it.

It is far too brief, but when we part at last, I can only stare up into his burning gaze. He is breathing raggedly just like me. I've said everything I cannot form into words in that kiss. If he asked me to stay again right now, I would say yes—brokenheart be damned.

Qurill remains silent as we stare at each other. With one thick swallow, I take a step back from him, missing his warmth immediately.

"Goodbye, Qurill."

My voice is a broken whisper. I don't want to let him see me cry. I turn quickly, nearly sliding in the sand. The walk along the beach is a tough battle. By the time I pause to catch my breath, I've barely started up the incline. I know it is foolish to do so, but I can't help myself.

There is a cracking pain in my chest as I stare at the beach. It's as empty as when we arrived. Qurill is gone, as is his boat. The only trace of him is the footprints in the sand that will soon be washed away by the tide.

Alone, I can finally crumble. A painful sob leaves my chest as my knees threaten to buckle. Each step feels like I'm walking through thick oatmeal. The top of the hill seems a thousand miles away. Agony slows my assent.

What's the point in any of this? All my life, I've been fighting so hard for something I don't even want. I've let fear control me. Those initial days of being alone made me retreat into myself. I've been too scared to live—to be selfish and claim the things that I want. I'm doing it again with Qurill now. The love of my lifetime just left me on the beach because I was too much of a coward to tell him I loved him.

I scream in frustration. Regret is a physical pain. Why did I let him leave? I may never see him again. How could I let him get away without telling him the truth? I owed it to both of us to say how I was feeling. So what if his devotion to me wanes? I need more time with him.

At least one more night.

Before I even realize it, I'm stumbling back down the hill at full speed. He told me I'd never find another to satisfy me, and he was right. I'll never give another my body as I gave to him. It was an innate sense to trust him. A primal part of me I didn't know I possessed wanted nothing more than to be owned by him.

He said he would come to me if I merely stripped down and waded into the water, calling his name. I can do that.

A figure sways into my path at the bottom of the hill. My heart surges thinking it is Qurill returning to me, but that elevation quickly ices over. The figure is dripping wet, dressed in dark rags. A sword hangs loosely from his hip. Scars decorate his sunburned face. His undershirt is ripped open, revealing faded ink atop his tan skin.

I recognize this man.

The single wave filled in with black ink on his chest signals that he is a part of Blacktide's crew. He is one of the men who helped Blacktide tie me to the rock. As he appears from the cliff's shadow, his poor state becomes apparent. He is missing a leather boot. A large chunk of missing flesh mars his temple. Crimson blood trails down the side of his face.

His gold tooth glimmers as he snarls at me. Quickly, brandishing his sword, he thrusts it forward. Instinctively, I hold up my hands. I can't make a run for it up the hill; even in his poor condition, he would catch me. I could try to scream, but there's no guarantee anyone milling about above would take me seriously before he had a chance to cut me down. I need to be patient and wait for him to make a mistake and rush for the sea.

If I can make it to the water, Qurill will save me. I know he will.

"I knew I'd find you here," the pirate snarls. "Saw that merman's boat with you aboard it—knew you were to blame."

I need to keep him talking. It's the only chance I have of him lowering his guard for even a moment.

"Sacrificing me to the Kraken was never going to work," I say. "The rough seas are an act of nature not even he can undo."

The pirate shakes his head, droplets of seawater flying.

"Damn the rough seas. That's not what I'm talking about."

I arch a brow.

"Then what am I to blame for now?"

"Blacktide is dead."

The sentence lands between us like a dead fish. My mouth falls open as goosebumps erupt on my flesh. The sun rises high overhead, beaming down on us with its full intensity.

"He's dead," the pirate repeats, "thanks to that merman. Strangled him right in front of all of us before sabotaging our hull. Everyone else is dead. I'm the soul survivor of the Dark Voyager, sent here to end you."

My mind is racing at the pirate's words. There is a chance he could be lying, but his appearance demonstrates that what he is saying is true. Qurill killed Captain Blacktide? He was so gentle with me, it's hard to imagine him doing something so bloodthirsty. And yet his words from yesterday float back to me.

And the man who chained you to this rock will be dead come sunrise.

A wicked thrill goes through me. I shouldn't be delighted by such violence, but knowing he did that all in the name of keeping me safe...how could I not love him?

Isn't this the confirmation I needed? He wouldn't send an entire pirate crew to their deaths over a casual lover. How could I ever think he would abandon me?

It's amazing how another brush with death can make everything seem clear.

"Your anger with me is misplaced," I say softly, taking a tentative step closer to the beach. "I have no knowledge of what the merman did."

His sword trembles in his grip. The sun glints off the deadly sharp blade. The blue water glimmers in the corner of my eye. So close and yet so far.

"You should be dead," he spits at me. "No matter. I'll sacrifice you myself. Gut you and throw you into the sea."

I scream as he jumps forward. I dodge just in time. The blade slices through the bodice of my dress, cutting through the padding of my corset. His dark eyes dance with madness. My slippers slide on the sand as I jump back. The sand cushions my back as I fall to the ground.

The pirate rights himself, gripping the sword in his hands and bringing it back. This blow will be more precise, and I won't be able to withstand it. I can't crawl fast enough to avoid the strike. I lift my hands, the only rudimentary shield I have.

I brace myself for the deathblow. Closing my eyes, I let the salty air and warm sun wash over me. My last moments alive, and just like before, I'm leaving this world with an insurmountable amount of regrets. I see Qurill's face in my mind, and I reach for it. He'll be waiting for me in the next life. I know it.

As the moments tick by, my death doesn't come. The sound of choking makes me blink my eyes open. They take a moment to adjust in the blinding sun. Once clear, I register the gruesome sight before me.

The pirate's hands hang limply at his side. His sword falls to the sand with a thud. Crimson pours from his stomach as a blue-scaled hand emerges covered in gore. Blood trails down his gasping mouth. Bile rushes up my throat at the sight, but I swallow it down.

Qurill is here.

Blue eyes rage as he growls down at the man in his grip. He bares his teeth at the pirate, and the man whimpers.

"It was a mistake coming after her," Qurill spits. "One you will pay for with your life. Just as your captain and the rest of your crew did."

In a flash, Qurill drags the man towards the water. The two

of them disappear into the depths. Finally aware of my body, I lurch up from the ground, my mind racing with all that's just happened.

I nearly died. Qurill has come back to me. I nearly died, and Qurill saved me yet again. He didn't abandon me. If I didn't think I could leave him before, I definitely cannot now. I rush towards the water. Waves wash over my slippers and soak the bottom half of my dress.

Calling out to my merman, I scan the horizon for any sign of him.

Finally, I see his familiar face breaking through the water. He is alone as he makes his way towards me. The pirate never emerges—another one of my enemies dealt with by the male I love. Desire for him pounds within me. The ache between my thighs is renewed the closer he gets.

I don't realize how much I'm shaking until Qurill reaches me and folds me into his strong arms. His large palms skim up and down my back as I burrow my face in his chest. His scent of sandalwood and citrus calms me. It is a balm to my fragile nerves. Tears pour down my cheeks as the weight of everything hits me.

Qurill hushes me softly, skimming his fingers through my hair. He places a soft kiss atop my head, tucking me under his chin.

"I'm so sorry, Astryd. I should've ensured they were all dead before I left you here."

I shake my head, pulling back to meet his eyes.

"You saved me," I whisper in awe. "Again."

A slight smile curves his lips.

"Always," he vows. "Even if you do not want me, I'll always be close by. Making sure you're safe."

My grip on him tightens, pulling our bodies flush together. There's no time for hesitating. Was this not a sign from the universe? Seems like I would be an even bigger fool to ignore a second brush with death. No more denials, no more half-truths. There is only space for truth in my life. No matter how scary it seems.

"Qurill, I do want you. I was coming back to the water to call out to you." My fingers skim up his naked torso. "To confess that I more than want you. I—I love you."

Qurill sucks in a shaky breath. I press on, afraid that if I stop, I'll lose my nerve.

"It was my mind telling me to leave you. I was afraid. I have been alone for so long—relying solely on myself—that I've forgotten what it means to trust someone. To have someone look out for you and make you a priority. I thought true happiness was peaceful solidarity. But you've shown me there's more to life. Why would I choose to live on the land when my heart already resides below the waves with you?"

Fresh tears skim down my cheeks. Qurill takes both thumbs and smooths them away.

"I love you too, Astryd. I'll love you forever." My heart is so full it feels as if it may burst. "My father fell for my mother in the same way. I did not need days or months to reach the conclusion I did the moment I met you. You are mine. Now and forever. My feelings for you will never wane—will only grow deeper the longer we spend together."

His lips brush my forehead.

"You will never be alone again," he vows. "I will protect you, provide for you, and show you all the wonders this world has to offer."

I giggle, tipping my chin up to catch his lips. Our mouths seal together as his hands clutch my head. Qurill trails open-mouth kisses along my neck and jaw.

"I'll give you more pleasure than your body can handle." Moisture slicks between my thighs at his words. "Each day, I'll claim you. Reminding you exactly who owns you."

"My body is yours," I moan. "As is my heart—my soul. You've owned every inch of me since we met."

I need him again. The only proper way to seal these vows is with our bodies. It's been too long since he was last inside of me. I need to feel him, or I might die. My hands fall to the sleeves of my gown. I rip my new dress clean down the middle and kick off my slippers. They float away on the tide. My corset floats away, followed by my shift until I'm naked in the morning sun.

My body heats under his hungry stare. His hand strays to my breast, palming it roughly.

"Take me here, Qurill. Now. I need you."

Qurill smiles wickedly at my words. His head swoops down to lick my puckered nipple. I groan and clutch at his arm. My body is on fire. The cool water caressing my ankles is my only reprieve. His mouth returns to mine, tonguing it just the way I like. I clench my thighs together, needing him to touch me there before I combust.

"If you want my cock," he purrs, breaking our kiss, "you know how I like you to ask for it."

I shiver at the commanding tone of his voice. My submission to him comes easily. It is an innate sense to give in to his dominance. It's an intoxicating feeling being able to give myself fully over to him. My guard isn't just lowered, it's gone.

There is no need for walls between me and the male I love. He owns me completely just as I own him. It is my submission that he craves, and giving it to him only heightens his pleasure. It is my power I wield that will bring us both to the highest peaks.

I smile demurely up to him, skimming my hands down his chest as I sink to my knees. He groans as I lean forward, trailing my tongue along the bulge in his leather pants. The salty taste enlivens my senses. Pulling back, I bite my lip and blink wide eyes up at him.

"Can I have your cock, my love? Please. I want it so bad."

Qurill chuckles. He unties the lacings of his pants. They sag before dropping to the sand. His massive cock stands at attention. A drop of seed collects at the tip. His soft scales decorating the shaft gleam in the sun. My mouth waters, eager to take him as deep as I can.

Gripping his cock, Qurill smears his seed along my lips.

"Hmm," he hums low in his throat. "Have you been good enough to earn it?"

I nod eagerly, licking his seed from my mouth.

"Trying to leave me wasn't very good, was it, Astryd?" He shrugs. "Maybe I should punish you?"

I brace my hands on his thighs, dragging my tongue over the velvety head of his cock. I love the taste of him.

"Yes," I sigh. "Punish me."

Qurill grins, grasping my shoulders in his hands. He pushes me backwards slightly.

"On your hands and knees," he commands.

I do as he says without thinking. Water splashes as he settles behind me. I groan as he grips my ass. His tongue licks up my slit, stopping to swirl around my entrance. Clawing at the sand, I feel his tongue drift higher. I scream as his tongue dives into my ass.

The slick muscle pumps into my tightness, loosening it just enough for it to push deeper. His fingers are not idle on my hip as I feel them part me. One sinks into my pussy, followed swiftly by another. With his tongue in my ass and his fingers roughly fucking me, I am a mess of sensations. The pleasure is too decadent. Broken whimpers fall from my lips as he plays me expertly.

He pumps me over and over, each one of my muscles tightening. I thrash on the beach, trying my best to absorb everything he's throwing at me. My heart pounds roughly against my ribs.

Qurill's hand connects with my ass. Pain spreads across my skin.

"Come," he growls.

I break and shatter at his command. I scream his name, fucking back on his fingers and tongue. Arousal leaks from my pussy and coats his thrusting hand. My eyes are open, but the world around me is a blur.

Before I can catch my breath, I feel his cock at my entrance. He pushes slowly inside me, not stopping until he's fully sheathed inside. His scales scrape my inner walls. Sweat spills down my back as I try to keep myself upright. Qurill snatches my hair and curls it around his fist.

"Tightest cunt on land or sea," he growls.

I moan, words are beyond me.

"Louder." He smacks my ass again. "Let them hear you up in Watership."

I scream as he begins to fuck me in earnest. My breasts jostle at the force of his thrusts. Each time his hips come in contact with my spanked ass, I moan louder. The pain heightens my pleasure. My fingers tunnel into the wet sand. Using my knees, I push back on his thrusts, allowing him to fuck me deeper.

His hands hook around my hips to power into me.

"The merman's little fucktoy. Tight, wet—needs to be fucked regularly. You thought I could leave you? Leave this perfect pussy without a cock to fill it?"

"Qurill," I choke, my vision darkening.

"You need me to own you. Don't you?" I nod, but he pulls my hair, pain breaking out along my scalp. "Say it."

"Yes, yes! You own me."

"Good girl," he praises. "Now come on my cock. Cover it in your sweetness. It'll need to be nice and slick to fit in your little ass."

He cock brushes a spot deep inside of me that makes me scream. The sound of our coupling echoes between the two cliffs. My pussy locks around his cock as I climax. Arousal pours from my entrance, soaking him in earnest. My back bows as pleasure erupts along my skin. I am nothing more than a trembling sensation.

Qurill slowly withdraws from my body. Voices grow louder, coming down from the top of the hill. No doubt someone has heard us; it sounds as if I'm being murdered down here. I pay it little mind. The whole town can watch for all I care.

Spreading my cheeks, Qurill spears his tongue into my ass, and I groan. He spits onto my unused hole as the head of his cock presses against me. Taking him into my pussy the first time had been intense. This is an even tighter fit. My ring of muscles seems hesitant to let him through. My body tries to relax, his determined invasion unhinges my jaw. My arms feel like jelly.

They can no longer support me, and my chest falls to the sand. Qurill grips my hips, keeping me aloft as he continues to slide in. He stretches me past the point of pleasure-pain. The sensation is like nothing I've experienced before.

"Take it," he snarls. "Take your punishment like a good girl."

I babble incoherently. His first thrust seems to go on forever, but eventually I feel his hips snug against my ass. My whole body trembles as I'm impaled on his hard cock. I've never felt so full in my life. There is no separating us. He has marked me inside and out. I wear his bruises and his teeth marks. Inside me, he's coated me in his come. Every inch of my body is his, and every piece of my heart belongs to him.

Qurill kiss along my spine. His heart pounds in time with mine. We've claimed each other. Our souls weave together as one in an unbreakable web. Our love is tangible. I reach for it on the beach. It envelopes me like an embrace. It is warm and all-consuming. Our love tastes of honey and feels like sunshine.

"I love you, Astryd. Let me show you how much."

I groan as he snatches me up. His cock is still lodged deep inside me. Hooking me around my elbows, he binds my arms behind my back. They are trapped against his chest. My knees bear my weight as he scoops his hips down slightly and then slides back into me.

His teeth sink into my earlobe. Qurill's cock withdraws before powering back into me. My teeth clench at the onslaught of pleasure.

"You are mine," he snarls in my ear. "Even if you try to leave me again, I'll find you. I'll drag you right back to this spot and fuck you until you vow to be mine again."

He slams into me, my pussy clenching around nothing.

"Never," I sob. "I'll never leave you."

"Perfect," he praises. "Your tight ass is going to make me come."

Pleasure washes over me at the thought of bringing about his peak. With a new goal looming, I clench my muscles around his thrusting cock. Qurill groans, his teeth sink into my shoulder. I delight in wearing another one of his marks.

"Come inside me, Qurill. Claim all my holes with your seed. Please."

His fingers find my clit, rubbing tight circles on it. My breath catches, and my pleasure looms. This one will unmake me. After this climax, I'll be reborn. My old life is over. There is only Qurill—only us. No more working, no more lonely nights filled with uncertainty. There will be adventures and pleasure and love—so much of it it seems impossible to fathom.

"Tell me what I want to hear, Astryd, and I'll reward your ass with my seed."

His fingers press harder against my clit. His other hand cups my breasts and pinches my nipple. I turn my head and lock eyes with him over my shoulder. I lay bare my soul to him, and I see that same devotion reflected back at me.

"I love you, Qurill."

Leaning forward, I capture his mouth as my body erupts. We groan into each other's mouths as we find our peaks at the same time. My hips freeze as my muscles lock down. Flames lick at my skin as bliss pools inside my stomach. Qurill jerks behind me, and hot seed floods my ass. He fucks it into my depths, each torrent heightening my climax.

Seed spills down my thighs as he finally withdraws. He turns me in his arms. Falling against his chest, he lands on his back atop the sand. The tide splashes along our sweaty bodies. The scent of our coupling hangs heavy in the air. His hands trail down my back and squeeze my ass. Satisfaction kindles in his gaze.

Placing a chaste kiss on his lips, I revel in this perfect moment. The sound of rushing water nearly lulls me to sleep.

"How are you feeling?" he asks gently.

"Wonderful." I smile. "Everything is perfect now that I have you."

"You're what's perfect." He kisses me again. "I love you so much, Astryd. My heart and soul. My mate. Let me prove myself to you. You've given me the greatest gift in agreeing to be mine—I'll never give you cause to regret it."

I open my mouth only to hear a shocked gasp from just beside us.

Glancing across the beach, I can't help but laugh at the small group of villagers collected there. They are all dressed in simple gowns and trousers. They each wear matching shocked expressions. Turning towards Qurill, I take his lips once again.

"Thanks for saving me again." I hook my arms around his neck. "Now take me home. We've given them enough of a show."

Leaning up, I nip at his ear.

"I want to reward my savior in our bed."

Qurill grips me to him. His smile is pure satisfaction.

"With pleasure."

7

ASTRYD

My steps slow on the gold vein marble.

Smoothing my seafoam colored dress, I can't seem to keep my palms from sweating. With it snug inside Qurill's strong grip, I must also be dampening his hand. I'd feel embarrassed for my errant perspiration if my nerves weren't at an all-time high.

Glancing over to Qurill, my merman is the picture of perfect confidence. Blue linen pants cling to his muscular thighs, while a matching shirt decorated with gold thread stretches across his upper body. He is dressed nicer than I've seen him. Though, to be fair, in the five days since our reunion on the beach, we've scarcely worn any clothes.

His hunger for me is rivaled only by my hunger for him. Every time he takes me, a deeper well of pleasure is unlocked. Qurill has claimed all of me. We've fucked in every room—every corridor—of Sunshell Palace. My screams of pleasure have scattered schools of fish. My body is an homage to his lovemaking.

Bruises in the shape of fingertips decorate my hips, while the imprint of his teeth adorns my neck and shoulders. I wear his marks proudly. They are a reminder of our love—that we've chosen each other. The endless days of solidarity are far behind us.

I'll never regret my choice in staying with him. Fear had stopped me from claiming what I truly wanted. Qurill keeps me safe. He alleviates all my concerns. Every time we come together, he tells me how much he adores me. Each morning, we share words of love and end each day in the same manner. Our love is permanent and unwavering.

The rare times we are not reveling in each other's embrace, we explore the surrounding sea. He shows me even more of his hidden coves and treasures lost to the water. My meals are succulent and shared with my lover. Still, my hunger is truly satisfied only once Qurill is inside me.

We are ravenous for each other, only refraining from taking each other out of necessity. And today is very much a necessity.

The Kraken of the Darksea's palace is magnificent. The polished marble floors pair with distinguished golden pillars. Large statues of forgotten deities and sea creatures line the hallway, pointing towards the glass ceiling. Like Sunshell Palace, all the water has been pumped out of the structure, making it suitable for a human to live here.

Not just any human—Qurill's mother, the Queen of the Darksea, lives inside the towering structure. All the surrounding grandeur makes my feet slide to a halt on the floor. My heart pounds and my thoughts race.

Qurill pauses beside me. Dropping my hand, he tips my face up to meet his gaze. The tenderness swimming in his blue eyes makes my knees weak. A simple golden circlet is woven between his white strands of hair. It glints in the warm light streaming in from above.

"What is wrong?"

Biting my lip, I shake my head, gesturing towards the large marble doors at the end of the hallway.

"What if they don't like me? Think I'm not suitable?" I say in a rush. "What if they think you've chosen poorly? What—"

"Astryd."

"I mean, it's not like I have much. I'm just a mediocre baker at best—no real skills, no family, no money. And you're a prince. A *prince*. Surely they will—"

His lips swoop down to capture mine. The firm press sets my blood on fire. His hand strays to my hair, careful not to destroy the artful twist keeping the top half away from my face. I melt against him. My hands curl against his chest, pulling him closer to me.

He tastes like salt—he tastes like forever.

"Firstly, you're not *just* anything," he says, breaking our kiss. "You are mine. My Astryd. My brave, passionate, and beautiful Astryd. My parents will adore you and wonder what you're doing with their irresponsible son."

Humor glimmers in his eyes, and I can't help but giggle.

"Irresponsible? What a cruel charge to lay against you."

He flattens his hand against mine, bracketing his chest.

"Nothing wounds a child more than the cutting condemnation of a parent."

I grin up at him, shaking my head. My breathing slows as calmness settles around the two of us. Qurill touches my cheek.

"They will love you—just as I do. Never doubt that."

My heart glows, and the threads of our souls weave together. I nod, kissing him again for strength before taking his hand again. Together we walk down the hall. The large marble doors are carved with two golden starfish. They groan as they peel back, revealing the staggering throne room.

A breath stills in my lungs at the opulent sight. Sparkling marble floors sprawl outward. The dais is made of the same glowing stone. Golden veining runs along the walls and wraps around the imposing columns. Blue silk dangles from the atrium above.

The massive throne is composed of golden tentacles, frozen in different fluid positions. Light pours in from the large windows behind the dais. The farther Qurill and I walk, the more beautiful everything becomes. The scent of citrus and jasmine floats in the air.

My eyes are eager to take everything in, but they are transfixed on the two figures before us.

The Kraken of the Darksea reclines against his massive throne. The blue hue of his skin matches that of his son's. Where Qurill is covered in delicate scales, the Kraken is all slick skin. It glistens with a glittering secretion. He's taken on a more humanoid form. Strong legs are braced on the marble floor. Short tentacles cascade down from his face.

He is a fearsome sight, but my eyes can't help but wander to the human woman draped in his lap.

Vibrant red hair curls down her back. Her thick strands are held back by a spectacular pearl crown. A dark blue gown clings to her petite frame. Freckled arms weave through her husband's short tentacles. Qurill has his mother's expressive, blue eyes. They shine with curiosity as she watches us approach. Her pink lips pull into a wide grin.

Gracefully, she slides from her husband's lap. One of his tentacles clings to her arm and tangles in her hair. She looks barely older than I do, yet there is a practiced fluidity in her movements. An ageless grace colors her features. She may look human, but she is just as otherworldly as her husband.

"My son," she calls.

Descending the dais, she extends her arm. She is a few inches shorter than I am. Qurill stoops down to embrace his mother. She lets out a content maternal sigh as she rubs gentle circles on his back.

The Kraken is hot on her heels as he comes up behind his wife. This close to me, I can barely register just how tall he is.

My eyes try to remain fixed on his, but are entranced by his wriggling tentacles that float on an invisible stream.

"You've been away too long." The Kraken of the Darksea's voice is commanding. "Your mother has been worried."

The Kraken claps his son on the shoulder once his mother releases him. The Queen of the Darksea playfully swats at her husband while rolling her eyes.

"Oh, hush. He is here now." Her blue eyes drift towards me, and I try my best not to cower. "And he's brought someone."

The full weight of both King and Queen's stares makes a sweat break out along my neck. I try not to fidget and look confident. I straighten my spine. Reining in my breathing is no easy task, but I manage it.

Qurill's hand finds my trembling one in the fall of my skirt. He interlocks our fingers and draws me into his side. I feel calm at once, his presence steadying me.

"Mother—father—this is Astryd." His hand grips mine. "My mate."

Both his parents gasp softly, their eyes going wide. They each exchange a subtle look before turning back towards me. I squeeze Qurill's hand back, wanting more than anything to make a good impression. I smile softly, shoving my nerves away.

"It is very nice to meet you both." I bow my head slightly before raising it again. "Your son saved my life—more than once. He is very brave, and I love him very much."

I hold my breath as I watch my words wash over them. The King and Queen share another look, longer than the last. Both come away smiling. Qurill's mother's eyes are glossy. Her freckled cheeks stretch as she smiles at me.

"My dear," she sighs, wrapping me in her arms. "Welcome home."

Qurill drops my hand so that I may properly embrace his mother. Despite our height difference and our similar appearance in age, this hug is that of a mother. It makes my heart ache remembering my own mother. She would be happy for me—she was always a dreamer and a believer in true love.

Tears sting my eyes as I hold on tighter to the Queen.

"Thank you, your majesty," I whisper, my voice near breaking.

The Queen laughs. Her slight shoulders shake as she pulls back. Squeezing my arms, her grin is infectious.

"Please, no formalities amongst family. You must call me, Melody."

Family. The word clangs through me.

The Queen—Melody—finally releases me. She grips her husband's hand and pulls him up beside her.

"And this is Zalenyk."

The Kraken offers me a warm smile. He squeezes my shoulder as he had his son before taking his wife in his arms. His tentacles play in her hair and suck lightly on her face. I find Qurill's hand again and lock our fingers tight.

"We are so happy to finally meet you." His eyes sparkle in amusement. "You are far too lovely for our reckless son."

"Zalenyk!" Melody reprimands, elbowing him in the stomach.

"Thanks for that, Father."

Qurill shakes his head, but he is grinning all the same. I can't help but join in their amusement. Life is easy. They approve of me and have welcomed me into their home. Everything is just as it should be.

"We've had some food prepared. You must be hungry after your journey here."

Zalenyk and Melody exit the throne room first. I turn to follow, but Qurill tugs my hand. His palms fall to my hips, turning me fully towards him.

"See, told you they'd love you."

I grin up at him.

"Right as always."

His lips brush mine in a featherlight touch. I groan, reaching for him again. Qurill chuckles against my lips, kissing me firmly once more before pulling back.

"I can't wait until we're alone," he confesses.

"Me as well."

His finger trails along my jaw.

"I've always dreamed of fucking my mate in my childhood bedroom." The low, decadent whisper of his voice causes me to shiver. "It's on the opposite side of the castle—no one will hear your screams of pleasure. Not unless I want them to."

Smiling against his mouth, I shake my head.

"You are incorrigible," I chastise.

"And you are mine."

"Forever."

"Forever," he agrees, sealing our eternity with one bruising kiss.

EPILOGUE
QURILL - TEN YEARS LATER

I'm not even sure the fucking plant is here.

Wading through itchy grass that grazes my calf, I try to breathe through the heavy pollen. The afternoon sun beats down on me. My gills twitch, longing for the water just like I am. Around me, the dense treeline of *The Woods* seems impenetrable. How I even found my way through to this pasture hardly seems feasible.

A mate's instinct to provide will take him anywhere, it would seem.

My heart squeezes at the thought of her: my Astryd. I've been away from her for too long, but she is the reason I'm wandering through this horrid grass. I need to find the herb the healer recommended. The algae and seagrass aren't helping her the way that they should.

Whatever my mate needs, she will always have—especially now.

My mate has only gotten more exceptional over the years. Those first few heady months were wonderful, but paled in comparison to what these past years have been like. We've explored every sea and made memories in every cove and on every beach. We've learned everything about each other. I keep all her secrets just as she does mine.

We can finish each other's sentences and convey a feeling with a shared glance.

I've lost track of the number of times I've taken her. Every day we revel in each other's embrace, one bout of lovemaking quickly devolving into another and another until the sun begins to rise. I can make her come with the slightest touch of my hand if I wish to. I know her body better than I know the sea.

It's why I was the first to notice when it began to change.

The idea of having a child had taken us both time to grapple with. There were a few years when we thought we were content to never have one. I was greedy for her back then—too selfish to allow anyone, even our child, to steal her time away from me. Our adventures wouldn't have been conducive to a newborn, and Astryd had wanted to see everything the world had to offer.

Then, in the last year, something shifted. A desire bloomed within us both to embark on a new adventure. I was ready to share her and expand our family as my parents had done with me. We hadn't been trying for very long, though, with my penchant for coming inside her whenever the opportunity arose, it was just a matter of time.

I took note of the new fullness to her breasts immediately. They fit my palm perfectly, until they suddenly started spilling over. That is when we both realized her courses had been absent for quite some time.

Now, Astryd was only a few months along. Her stomach was only curved slightly, but she glowed from within as if the sun resided in her heart. It seems an impossible feat for her to have gotten more beautiful, but while she's been pregnant, I sometimes find it hard to look at her for too long. Her loveliness causes me physical pain. One that demands I keep her chained to our bed so I can make love to her until the baby comes.

Astryd has told me I cannot do that, so I have to keep my primal urges to myself for now. She tells me it's important for both of us to keep busy, but this errand feels pointless the more hours I spend away from her. I know I cannot return empty-handed. These first few months of pregnancy have not been easy on my sweet mate. Astryd hasn't been able to keep any food down. My mother's remedies worked for a time, but she's begun to throw those up as well.

Therefore, I need to find the *wyldroot* to help settle her stomach. It has to be around here somewhere. A sneeze makes my already burning eyes water more. I sweep at the insects flying in the air. I nearly choke on the scent of cedar and dirt.

Apprehension tickles my neck, and I pause my searching. Behind me, heavy footsteps fall, followed by a deep growl. I silently curse at myself. Why had it not crossed my mind that this land could belong to another creature?

Taking a deep breath, I slowly turn around to learn what has crept into the pasture with me. Long horns, the color of a midnight sky, gleam. Their deadly sharp points reach towards the sun. Large nostrils flex as its muzzle pulls back in warning.

The creature is over seven feet tall. It stands ready to spring on two heavily muscular legs that taper into thick hooves. Impressive arms cross over an equally impressive chest as the creature cups its long fingers around its elbows.

Minotaurs are imposing figures this close up.

"You shouldn't be here," it snarls. "This land is mine."

His deep voice nearly makes my knees buckle, but I hold firm. Astryd's face grounds me and gives me the strength to press on. I hold up my hands to indicate I am no threat to him. He could gore me with those impressive horns in an instant. This far from the water, my magic hardly makes a difference.

"I'm looking for *wyldroot*. My mate is sick." Something

flashes in the creature's dark eyes, but he shakes himself. "If you would guide me to it, I'll be on my way."

The minotaur's nostrils flare again with a heavy huff. His muscles loosen slightly, but he still doesn't look friendly. After what feels like an eternity, he waves his hand towards my right.

"Under that oak tree, you'll find some growing along the base." He bears his teeth for good measure. "Take it and be gone."

He doesn't have to tell me twice. Relief instantly floods me.

"Thank you," I say with a swift nod.

Walking to the base of the tree, I harvest as much of the green-colored root as I can. The blue flowers guide me to their thick stems, which hold the medicine Astryd needs. I take the jars out of my satchel and quickly fill all three large containers. Once I'm satisfied I have enough—and not relying on the minotaur's fleeting goodwill if I need to procure more—I nod my thanks again and walk quickly from the clearing and into *The Woods*.

I feel the creature's eyes on me the entire time. I pity the poor soul whose path crosses with that beast next.

The sound of rushing water makes me sigh with relief. A foaming spring bubbles over jagged rocks. Double-checking the containers of *wyldroot* are secure, I leap into the water. Its calming, cool surrounds me, replenishing me in an instant. I dive deep and follow the small stream until it finally feeds into the sea.

I glide through the water with ease. My arms and legs pump as Sunshell Palace comes into view. I'm more eager than ever to see Astryd. Hopefully, this *wyldroot* will help soothe her stomach. I say a silent prayer as I burst through the water bubble and splash onto the tile floor of the entryway.

Grabbing a towel, I sponge the water from my body as I make my way towards our bedroom. I left her sleeping this morning, and that's where she's remained. The babe has stolen most of her energy. Quietly, I open the doors to our room. My blood heats at the sight of her on the bed.

Golden lashes lay atop her rosy cheeks. Her supple body is visible beneath her thin white nightgown. The silk hugs her curves, highlighting her growing stomach. I quietly set the satchel on the bed before leaning down to press a kiss to her smooth brow.

Sleepy blue eyes blink up at me. Her lips pull into a smile. A soft finger runs along the water still drying on my shoulder.

"Where have you been?" she asks, voice thick with sleep.

"Out. Getting this."

Reaching into the bag, I take out one of the jars of *wyldroot*. Her eyes go wide as she sits up in bed. Taking the jar, she examines it before catching my eyes again. Love swims in her crystal eyes.

"You are the perfect mate."

I chuckle as I reach for her glass of water. Twisting off the lid, I use a small knife to slice through the root's center. I scrape as much of the inner sticky membrane into her water as I can. Mixing it around, the clear water quickly turns deep navy.

Astryd takes the glass, grimacing at the taste of the *wyldroot*. She drinks down the liquid in one go. I set her discarded cup to the side as she breathes deeply, a casual hand falling on her stomach.

"How do you feel?"

I hold my breath as she tilts her head to the side.

"Better," she says finally. I sag with relief. "I woke up nauseous, but the effect of the *wyldroot* is nearly instant."

"Are you hungry?"

She shakes her head. A yawn sneaks up on her.

"This baby is stealing all my energy. I feel like I've been sleeping the days away."

I tuck a piece of golden hair behind her ear. My love for her surges. To know that I have provided for her inflames my male pride.

"Rest," I command. "I'll lie beside you."

Fire burns in her gaze. A small smile curves her lips. Heat flares inside of me. I can see the wicked thoughts unraveling through her head. Astryd's nipples pebble along the front of her nightgown.

"I'd love for you to join me in bed," she whispers. "But not to sleep."

I groan as her hands fall to the thin straps of her nightgown. With two quick tugs, the material falls from her chest and collects at her waist. Her large breasts rise and fall with her rapid breathing. Color erupts on her golden flesh.

"Are you certain?"

Even as I ask the question, I'm already rising from the bed. My cock is hard as steel. Shucking my pants off is no easy task around my straining length. Astryd's eyes turn glassy, licking her lips at the sight of my cock.

She nods, her thighs rubbing together beneath sheets. Coming down on top of her, I brace the majority of my weight on my elbows. She moans as my mouth finds hers. Our kiss is claiming. It starts slow but quickly turns frantic as if centuries have kept us apart rather than a handful of hours. Her blunt nails score down my back, making me nip at her lip.

The pregnancy has made her desire for me even more rampant. A feat that, along with her increased beauty, I didn't think possible. Yet, I am continuously awoken in the night by her gorgeous body atop mine. She works me in her sleep, rubbing her wet pussy against my cock until we both come fully awake. That's when she begs me with a pout to roll her over and fuck her thoroughly.

I'm all too happy to oblige her pleasure whenever it surfaces. She has given herself to me, and I will see to each and every one of her needs without question. I've never given her a moment to waver in her choice to be with me. We have each other forever.

Her mewls against me tell me she's already close. Astryd's thighs snag around my hips, dragging her cunt along my cock. I reach between us to slap it down on her clit. She moans, throwing her head back in bliss. I take her open mouth as an invitation to spear my tongue into.

As much as I'd love nothing more than to sink into her heat and feel her come around my cock, I wish to take my time with her. Thoughts of the past urge me to slow this moment down and enjoy my mate's wanton nature.

My fingers sink into her nightgown as we kiss. With a tug, I rip it the rest of the way off her body. She moans into my mouth, shivering against me. Kissing down her jaw, I tear her nightgown into strips. She is unaware of my goal as she turns her neck for me to suck at her throat.

With her waist in my palms, I gently push her up the bed. Her back is cushioned against the pillows as I return to her lips.

"Are you going to be a good girl and obey me? She nods frantically. "Then keep still."

Her breath catches as I lift both her delicate arms towards the headboard. Using the strips of silk, I gently bind her to it. Her chest rises and falls. I can see and scent the arousal slipping down her thighs. Her body is on full display—a feast for only me to enjoy.

I kiss her lips, my hand falling to her breast. She moans as I squeeze.

"This is just how I found you. Bound to that rock, completely at my mercy. Waiting for me to claim you—my little sacrifice."

"Qurill," she sighs as I lick her other nipple.

"This is when you are at your most beautiful, Astryd. Bare to me. Your body is mine for the taking, however I see fit. Whether it is your mouth I choose to fuck—or your perfect pussy or even your tight little ass—the choice is mine. Isn't it?"

I tease her nipple with my teeth, and she screams. Her legs scissor on the bed, desperate for any kind of relief.

"Yes, always yours. Please, Qurill."

My smile curves along her soft skin.

"And do you know why that is? Do you know why you've given yourself to me so freely—even in the beginning?" My mouth finds her ear and licks the tender shell. "It is because you know your pleasure is paramount. I'm in control of you because I'm the only one who gets to see you like this. Who gets to taste you and fuck you and make you come until your body gives out."

She gasps at my words. The truth of them settles into my bones. I may control her body, but she owns me completely. Everything I do is in service to her. I can't breathe without her. Our love is a tangible thing that flows between us, deepening our desire.

"Please, I need you."

I laugh against her, my hand trailing between her breasts. It stops atop her stomach for a moment, caressing gently before trailing lower.

"I know what you need, sweet sacrifice."

My fingers skim up her dripping slit. Her thighs open as far as they can. I cup her for a moment, enjoying how wet and warm she is. My thumb works her clit as she moans, but stops before she can erupt. Her angry groan breaks off in a scream as I sheath two fingers deep inside her.

I fuck her roughly with my fingers. Astryd yanks at her restraints as her whole body goes taut. Her eyes are open, but I know she can't see me. I curl my fingers inside her, hitting the spot I know will make her erupt.

And erupt she does. Screaming my name, she comes on my hand. Her arousal splashes up my wrists as her clenching pussy locks down on me. I don't stop, not even as she trembles. My mouth falls to her breast, laying open-mouth kisses against each soft mound. I tongue her nipples, alternating between biting and sucking them.

My fingers fuck her faster, giving her no reprieve. Her breath catches as I feel her start to tighten up once more.

"Again. Come on my fingers again, Astryd. Soak the sheets."

She moans, her hair fanning out behind her on the pillow. Her pulse quivers in her neck. Scarlet blooms across her cheeks and chest.

"I—I don't know if I can take it. Another one."

Her words are choppy, her plea only half-hearted. I don't slow down, merely renew my teeth marks on her breast.

"You asked me for pleasure. If you really want me to stop, you know what to say."

I wait for her to utter the word that will have me untying her and holding her to me in a heartbeat. Warring thoughts filter over her gorgeous face, yet her lips remain closed. I know what she wants—what she needs—more than she does. Astryd needs her limits pushed, and I'm the only male who can do it.

Crawling down her body, I suck her throbbing clit into my mouth. Her sweetness coats my tongue instantly. The headboard groans as she pulls against her bindings. Trembling thighs graze my ears as I feast from her in time with my fingers. I lick her as she continues to shake.

Pulling my fingers free, I quickly replace them with my tongue. My slick fingers slide into her ass easily, and I know she is done for. Astryd's mouth opens on a silent scream as she soaks my face. I lick up every delicious drop of her spend. Rubbing my face in her wetness, I'm completely coated in her.

Rising over her, I spear my cock into her pink cunt. Her orgasm makes her even tighter than she usually is. I relish the tight hold of her muscles as I ruthlessly fuck her. My hands fall to her hips, dragging her down my length in time with my pounding. No doubt my fingertip bruises will be renewed on her flesh.

Our bodies slap together in a symphony of love. She's tightening down on me before long. Her climax is swift and surprising. My body urges me to come with her, but I hold off, biting down on my lip until I taste blood.

Sweat coats her body as I pull out of her. Carefully, I slide beneath her. Hoisting her up, she aids me by keeping herself on her feet as I position my dripping cockhead at her entrance. With her hands still bound, she is still at my mercy. All she can do is withstand my fucking and keep her balance.

"So good. You feel so good inside me."

Her words are slurred with pleasure.

The soft globes of her ass land on my hips with satisfying smacks. Her breasts bounce in time with my thrusts. Each impact of our bodies makes my blood boil. I need to give her my seed. The urge to fill her again is all-consuming.

Reaching up, I sever her bonds. Her hands fall to my chest, biting into my scales. I lick the sweat from her spine and wrap her golden hair around my fist. She keeps pace while she rides me. Her expert hips work me just the way I like. The look of pleasure she gives me over her shoulder seals her fate.

My hand reaches around her hip, finding her clit.

"I'm close, my love. Please. I need your seed inside me. I want it."

Snatching her hair back until I know she feels the burn, I growl against her shoulder.

"Then clench that sweet pussy down on me one more time, and I'll fill you up good and deep."

I pound into her once, twice, and then she erupts again. Her pussy locks me down, and I thrust forward, emptying myself into her depths. I bathe her inner walls in my come. Fucking every last drop I have into her. I let go of her hair as her trembling body falls back against my chest.

Rolling us to our sides, I kiss her lips and damp brow. She smiles up at me, her eyes already turning heavy. Reaching between us, I go to pull out of her when a gentle hand stops me.

"Let's stay like this for a while. I like feeling full of you."

"Isn't our child already providing you with that sensation?"

Astryd rolls her eyes, smacking at my shoulder with a smile.

"It's not at all the same thing."

My hand falls to her stomach. Beneath the gentle curve, there is a life growing inside her. We don't know what our child will look like. My parents had believed I'd be made of tentacles like my father. This form was different than what they could've ever anticipated, and I have a feeling Astryd and I will be experiencing the same thing.

Our child could have fangs and a tail, and I would love it just as I know she would.

We smile tenderly at each other. Her hand comes down over mine as we cradle our child resting inside her.

"The baby will be here before we know it," Astryd whispers.

I kiss her temple.

"Then I should savor all your attention while I still have it."

Her laugh is sweeter than the sound of crashing waves.

"You'll live. He or she will steal your attention, too. That is the plight of all parents."

Life with Asryd is unbelievably perfect. It is inconceivable to think that we may not have met. If fate hadn't put her on my horizon, I wouldn't be here with her.

The future ahead of us is bright and filled with so much love. There is no place for fear or uncertainty when the fabric of our souls has become one. We will never know what life is like without the other.

As long as she stays below the waves, my father's magic will keep her in eternal youth just as he had done for my mother. Forever doesn't seem as daunting when you have someone to share it with.

"Sleep while you can, mate." I nuzzle into her neck. "I'll want to fuck you again soon."

"With pleasure."

I tuck her head beneath my chin. Her soft hair tickles my face as her small hands curl against my chest. Almost instantly, sleep claims her. My hands skim down her bare back as I hold her close. Our hearts beat together as one.

Fate brought us together, and I thank my good fortune for it every day. She was always meant to be mine. My Astryd, my mate, and soon-to-be the mother of my child. The future will certainly be something we'll both have to navigate, but one thing remains true:

Our love is as permanent and unending as the sea.

DON'T MISS THE NEXT ONE!

The second volume of the beloved Kiss From a Monster series is coming April 2026! Read novellas 5-8 that contain brand new bonus scenes. Pre-order today!

The ninth book in the series is coming! Pre-order today. A lonely minotaur meets the human woman who will change his life forever. Coming Summer 2026!

READ ME OTHER BOOKS!

Interconnected monster romance standalone on Kindle Unlimited!

Short and spicy monster romance novellas following a different diabolical looking creature!

Holiday-themed monster romances for those who want a little extra spice on Kindle Unlimited!

ACKNOWLEDGMENTS

I want to thank all of you for picking up *A Kiss From a Merman*! I hope you all enjoyed our dominant merman and the woman who ensnared his heart. Would you like to see more from Astryd and Qurill? A bonus scene of them will be future in my collection book, *Kiss From a Monster Series Volume 2*, coming next month!

I'd like to thank my beta/ARC teams, my patrons, and all of you who've shared or continue to support my work. See you in the next one!

xoxo Charlotte

ABOUT THE AUTHOR

Charlotte Swan is twenty-seven year old, living in Chicago. When she is not dreaming about being whisked away to a world filled with magic and sexy monsters, she is busy being a freelance social media marketer and full-time smut lover. To read her debut novel *Taken by the Dark Elf King*, hear about her upcoming projects, or to connect with her on social media please find her on her website or by scanning the code below.

www.authorcharlotteswan.com